MISUNDERSTOOD MEG

MAIL ORDER BRIDES RESCUE SERIES, BOOK #4

JO GRAFFORD, WRITING AS JOVIE GRACE

Copyright © 2019 by Jo Grafford, writing as Jovie Grace

All rights reserved.

No part of this book may be reproduced in any form without written permission from the author or publisher, except as permitted by U.S. copyright law.

ISBN: 978-1-63907-018-3

GET A FREE BOOK!

Join my mailing list to be the first to know about new releases, free books, special discount prices, Bonus Content, and giveaways.

https://BookHip.com/GNVABPD

ACKNOWLEDGMENTS

An enormous thank you to my beta readers and editor, Cathleen Weaver, for sharing their thoughts and insight about this story. Also, I'm sending a huge shout-out to my Cuppa Jo Readers on Facebook for reading and loving my books!

ABOUT THIS SERIES

The only mail order bride company with an insurance policy enforced by the Gallant Rescue Society — *No extra cost!*

The Gallant Rescue Society Oath

"I hereby solemnly pledge my gun and my honor to the Gallant Rescue Society.

To be called upon day or night.

To rescue any Bride-To-Be from any undesirable circumstance on her journey to meet her Groom.

To return her (if at all possible) with her virtue intact to the Boomtown Mail Order Brides Company.

No questions asked.

So help me, God."

CHAPTER 1: QUEST FOR HAPPINESS

Margaret Vivienne Gladstone took one last walk around the near empty ballroom of her late father's palatial Boston mansion. She wasn't going to miss it — the endless parties, charity events, and other social obligations; the pressure to dress and act and talk just so; the endless pursuit of gossip columnists and newspaper reporters; and the crushing scrutiny of the social elite who'd never quite accepted her father for his lack of old family connections.

With the death of Herman Gladstone, owner and captain of Gladstone Trans-Atlantic Shipping — may her stern, hardworking father rest in peace! — she was a vastly wealthy heiress. Though the bulk of her inheritance was tied in legal knots she barely understood, contingent in some way upon her future marriage to some eligible bloke or another, her monthly allowance was substantial. In short, she was free to do anything she wished or go anywhere she pleased.

The new owners of the place she'd called home for the past eight years were scheduled to collect the keys from her attorney in the morning.

This was goodbye. She didn't bother looking back when the enormous double doors closed behind her. A hired carriage was waiting at the curb of the cobblestone street to carry her to a modest inn where she planned to eat a simple meal, stay in an average room, and be treated like an ordinary person.

For the first time in twenty-one years, she wouldn't have to be escorted by a squadron of bodyguards. The scepter to her father's mighty empire had been passed on to his business partner. She could no longer be used as a pawn by his enemies, as leverage to bend him to their will. She was free!

She would no longer have to be pointed at and whispered about as the pampered only daughter of a famed shipping baron. Her motherless state needn't be tsk'd about. The style of her gown didn't have to be exclaimed over, and the name of her dressmaker wouldn't have to be repeated a dozen or more times throughout dinner. Most importantly, she would not have to spend the evening listening to her future endlessly debated by perfect strangers nor her name paired in conversation with an exhaustive number of potential suitors from Boston to London.

Tonight, she intended to be Meg. Simply Meg.

She peered out the window of her carriage and drew the first easy breath she had in months. All necessary legal paperwork was signed and filed. Her father's estate, vehicles, and collectibles were sold. All his servants and every one of her bodyguards had been sent on their way with glowing letters of reference, and most were gainfully re-employed; she'd seen to that. Her life was now her own.

A late November wind whistled, and snow flurries fell on the pedestrians bustling down Broadway, leaving a thin layer of white dust on black top hats, felt bonnets, and raised parasols. The horses slowly clip-clopped their way past gilded buggies displaying family crests and an occasional sleek, black, horseless carriage. The main part of the city faded to the outskirts, and the accoutrements on the buildings became less ornate. The evening crowd thinned considerably.

Meg wasn't sure how much time passed — a half hour, maybe an hour — before her hired carriage turned down a hard-packed, earthen street. Here the pedestrians carried dinner pails as they trudged home from their places of work in well-worn trousers and boots. Most people walked. Only a few drove wagons, and those that did weren't carrying passengers. Their rigs were loaded with crates and barrels.

At last, Meg's driver reached the small country inn she'd so painstakingly researched. A courier earlier in the day had been sent to verify her reservation. It was a two-story building with roughly hewn plank walls and an honest-to-heavens thatched roof. Her excitement increased. She'd never slept under a grass ceiling before. A swirl of smoke rose from two slightly crooked chimneys, and candles winked charmingly in the front windows.

The team of horses slowed and halted before the front door. It was painted a minty green and peeling around the handle. A blue urn with a chipped rim rested at a slight angle on the front stoop, bearing the wilted remains of fall mums.

One moment her driver was helping her down from the high carriage, and the next moment she was enveloped by a small army of inn workers.

Young grooms clambered atop the carriage to remove her impressive pile of trunks along with the odd-and-end assortment of treasures she'd been unable to part with — an antique carousel horse her father had commissioned to be turned into a toy rocker when she was smaller, a mantle-sized portrait of her playing at the knees of a mother she had no memory of, and her favorite paint-spattered easel. She never went anywhere without her art supplies. There were brushes and canvases, a tall white column with a flat top where she did her sculpting, and a sewing machine she was still learning to use.

A stout couple in their middle years waited for her just inside the door of the inn.

"Madame Gladstone." The man treated to her a low, jerky bow that felt out of place somehow amid the cheery wooden tables and scattering of mismatched chairs that comprised the dining area. "We are honored and delighted you chose to patronize our humble establishment. I am Felix, and this is my wife, June."

The woman blushed a rosy pink and bobbed a curtsey. "Pleased to meet you, we are," she breathed, brushing a strand of salt-and-pepper hair away from her round face and smoothing it back into her bun. "We're placing you in our finest room, and our most skilled gel will be attending you."

Meg's heart sank in slow degrees as it dawned on her that she had not, in fact, driven far enough to escape her highborn reputation. To Felix and June, she was still the daughter of a late shipping mogul to be wined and dined with their finest dishes, bed linens, and service.

Instead of passing an evening in quiet anonymity as she'd so carefully planned, she found herself dining in a private, curtained-off alcove, away from the rest of the guests.

Instead of being served the mouth-watering pumpkin spice soup she could sniff in the air, they delivered her a side of veal swimming in rich sauces, potato dumplings, and a small tray of designer pastries she could only assume were purchased from a baker in the city.

The cheerful hubbub of voices outside the alcove made her part the curtains to peek at the world she'd been excluded from. Men in patched shirts and britches were hungrily spooning the pumpkin soup down as fast as the serving girls could ladle it. A young couple in travel clothes were valiantly attempting to soothe two whimpering babes while a pup nestled beneath their table whined for scraps.

Swallowing her loneliness, Meg crept to the nicest room in the inn, crawled beneath the owners' newest and cleanest bed linens, and blew out her candle. Clearly, she needed to come up with a better plan if she was ever going to break free of the confinements imposed by her privileged upbringing.

THE NEXT MORNING dawned cooler than the day before, providing the perfect excuse to trade in her silk mourning gown for her favorite emerald wool. Bundling a thick fur coat over it, she plunged her hands inside a pair of muffs and pronounced herself ready to depart.

A frigid wind swirled its way across the countryside as she instructed her driver to shuttle her from village to village. Alas, nothing but hunger pains struck as the morning ripened to noon. In the end, she found herself directing him to drive her back to Boston. She insisted on being let out on Main Street so she could walk. And think.

She wandered aimlessly past shop windows, cut through a small park with frozen turf, and strolled past monuments. With every step, she wished there was some place on earth she could go where nobody knew her, where she could start fresh. A place where she could put down roots, make friends, and build the kind of life she'd never known but always dreamed of.

On the corner of 14th Street and Broad, a brightly painted sign caught her eye. She stepped closer to read the gilded letters surrounded by a wreath of painted wildflowers.

Boomtown Mail Order Brides

That sounded strange. She wrinkled her nose at the

thought of a man ordering his bride through the mail. Who would do such a thing? It reeked of something downright scandalous! And yet...

Curiosity got the better of her. Since she was now free to do whatever she wanted, she pushed open the glass-paneled door and was charmed when the movement set off a tinkling bell rigged to the top of it.

A man in a navy business suit, who couldn't be too many years her senior, rose from his desk in the center of the room. He had a rangy build, longish brown hair, and a calm, assessing smile.

"Good afternoon, and welcome to the Boomtown Mail Order Brides Company." His subtle scrutiny of her emerald gown and long, fur coat pulled his mouth in a puzzled quirk. "I'm Jordan Branson." He stuck out a hand.

She hated giving her name, but it would be rude to withhold it. Maybe he wouldn't recognize her shortened version of it. "Meg Gladstone," she returned and shook his hand.

The immediate sharpening of his dark eyes told her he recognized it all too well. "How may I help you, Miss Gladstone?"

"Call me Meg, please." She was weary of pomp and titles. She swiftly scanned the room. It was an inviting place with blue and white striped chairs and lacy eyelet curtains. "Why would anyone sign a contract to marry a person they'd never met?" she mused. "When I read your sign, I couldn't resist coming inside to ask."

He gave a bark of laughter and swept one arm towards the striped chairs. "I am happy to answer your question and any others. Would you care to sit?"

She sat, unbuttoned her coat, and fanned her skirts around her knees.

"Tea?" He strode to a side bar and pulled out two floral teacups trimmed in gold.

"Yes, please."

He poured her a steamy concoction that smelled of cinnamon, nutmeg, and something a wee bit on the daring side.

He took a seat across from her, sipping from his own cup. "The ladies who walk through our front door usually want something very specific." He waved away the steam rising from his tea and set the cup down on a darkly painted end table. "Some wish to travel. Some hope to find better employment opportunities. Nearly all of them are seeking love, acceptance, and family."

Family. His words tightened around her heart like a hopeful fist and squeezed. There was nothing in the world she wanted more, yet it was the one thing her money couldn't buy. She opened her lips to ask a follow-up question but closed them without uttering a single word. *No.* What Mr. Branson was suggesting was utterly preposterous. Women walking into this establishment might indeed be seeking such lofty things, but no man possessed the power to make their wishes come true. If her father were present, he would insist this man's business was nothing more than a sham, structured to swindle starry-eyed hopefuls out of their hard-earned cash.

"Tell me." He leaned forward in his chair, resting his forearms on his knees and loosely clasping his well-manicured hands. "If you could paint a picture of the perfect life, what would it look like?"

Thoroughly intrigued by the question, she took another sip of tea, gathering the snippets of scenes swiftly forming in her mind. She could discuss art all day long. "Are we discussing the perfect life for me or someone else?"

He spread his hands. "How about we pretend you're painting this picture for a dear friend?"

"Very well." She cupped the warm teacup with both hands, breathing in its spicy scent, and closed her eyes. Her imagination had no trouble taking over. She knew exactly where she wanted to live, just not how to get there. It was a place she'd dreamed and daydreamed about her entire life. "I'm picturing a cozy little cottage with a front porch and a view of the mountains. Plus a rocker for sitting and enjoying the view. Of course, there would have to be a kitten or pup sunning on the stairs and a few horses grazing in the distance. I think there would also be a man nearby." She cocked her head sideways, trying to picture how she would paint him. "He has his sleeves rolled up, and he's chopping firewood. Not exactly handsome, and far from perfect, but a good man. An honest, hardworking one." She opened her eyes. "At the corner of my canvas, I would paint two small children playing in the grass in their bare feet. One is holding a rag doll in her arms, the other a wooden ball."

When she grew silent, Jordan Branson mused, "You're a painter."

She smiled. "Yes. How did you—?" Her eye caught a fleck of blue paint adhering to her fingernail. "Never mind."

"How would you title your painting?"

She grimaced. "True happiness." The scene she'd described contained every ounce of what she'd been missing while growing up, every drop of what was missing in her current circumstances.

"That's an interesting title. Why did you choose it?" he prodded.

She made a face at him. "Because it's a happy scene. There's fresh air and sunshine in it, something to do, someone to love..." Logic told her no such place existed. Though it went against her nature, her father had raised her to be pragmatic. Girls like her were painstakingly reared to make proper matches when they were older — to garner new business alliances, extend the family estate, and such. The world in her painting only existed in fairytales, but a girl could dream, couldn't she?

Mr. Branson stood and strode to his desk. "What if I could secure a ticket for you to visit such a place, Miss Meg?"

She spared him a sad smile. "Impossible!" Ah, what a charming swindler he was, though.

He shot her a half-curious, half-concerned look. "On the contrary, I received an application in the mail a few weeks ago that might be just the opportunity you're seeking." He lifted a folded letter and smoothed it open. "Here. You may read it for yourself." He returned to the sitting area and held it out to her with an innocent expression she was certain was intended to convince her he had nothing to hide.

Thoroughly bemused at this point, she laid down her teacup to accept it. Two things stood out to her right away. First of all, it was a typed letter, not a handwritten one. Secondly, it was printed on a fine grade of beige stationery and had been previously sealed with a coffee bean shade of wax, though she could no longer decipher the shape of the object imprinted on it now that the seal was broken.

"Hmm." She swiftly read its contents.

Mr. Branson:

A few months ago, I would have thought it foolish to pen such a letter. However, after witnessing your agency arrange three successful marriages in my town, I am forced to admit that a satisfying union is indeed possible through your less-than-conventional methods.

What I am hoping for in a bride is difficult to put into words, but your instructions were to paint a picture of the perfect wife, so I will do my best.

She is a woman of deep and abiding faith, kind-hearted and intelligent, someone able to see the beauty in every situation — no matter how bleak — as well as the beauty in others, a person who shares my insatiable thirst for learning and experiencing new things, someone who understands nothing worth having comes without a cost, a woman willing to take that risk by joining me in Arizona.

If you can find such a woman, I will marry her and cherish her for however long the good Lord will grant us together.

My deepest regards,
Shadrack Nicholson

"Oh-h-h!" Meg expelled the air in her lungs in one, long, breathy sigh. What a dreamy letter! "Is he a poet? He sounds like a poet."

"He's a telegraph clerk."

She wrinkled her nose. "A clerk?" It was a bit disappointing to learn the man who could spin words together like Browning was nothing more than a simple clerk.

"On weekdays, yes. He works on his farm most weekends and holidays."

"Ah." She pictured a tiny scrap of land with the start of a humble garden. "Is he trying to save up enough to farm full-time then?" Not that the plight of a humble farmer on the other side of the country was any concern of hers…

"Unlikely, since he already owns his homestead outright. His staff keeps it running while he is away."

What? She gaped at him. That made no sense. How could a lowly clerk not only afford his own farmlands but have deep enough pockets to hire others to manage it for him? She handed back Mr. Nicholson's letter, utterly mystified. "I confess I'm not certain I understand why you wished me to read his letter in the first place, Mr. Branson." She'd be wise to end their strange conversation *tout suite* and be on her way. The answers she was seeking wouldn't be found by spinning castles in the air with a would-be matchmaker.

"Call me Jordan." He gave her an easy smile. "What I'm

trying to do is answer your most burning question — the one you asked when you first walked through the door. Why would a man order a wife through the mail?" He shrugged. "There isn't a quick or an easy explanation. All I can tell you is Shadrach Nicholson owns a house on his farm with a clear view of the surrounding canyons and mesas. He also owns horses, cattle, sheep, chickens, and a pack of hunting dogs. I'm not entirely certain about the rocking chair on the front porch." His smiled broadened. "As yet, he has no children, but who knows what the future may hold?"

Meg's jaw dropped. "Did you just—?" No, it wasn't possible! Or was it? Unless she was mistaken, Jordan Branson had just pointed out the similarities between her painting depicting a perfect life and Mr. Nicholson's letter describing the perfect wife.

"Did I what?"

"I am trying to decide whether I am offended by your brazenness or impressed by your cleverness!" She yanked the lapels of her coat together, preparing to take her leave.

He stood and handed her a small white card bearing his contact information. "When you decide, you know where to find me, Meg."

CHAPTER 2: A GLAMOROUS ARRIVAL

"There." Shadrack Nicholson dusted his ink-stained hands and took a step away from the wonders of the telegraph machine he'd been demonstrating to his new protégé. "That's all there is to it." He surveyed the lanky beanpole of a lad, liking what he saw.

Bram Fairfield was the son of a hardworking miner in the newly incorporated Hopes Landing community that lay just outside the city limits of Headstone. He was nineteen, full of book learning, and eager to please. Alas, his attempt to follow in his father's footsteps had ended beneath a collapsed wall that rendered his left arm paralyzed.

Bram smoothed a hank of brown hair back from his forehead while a cautious smile tugged at the corners of his mouth. "You really think I can keep up with the workload around here, Mr. Nicholson?" He glanced ruefully down at the hand hanging limply against his faded but freshly pressed gray trousers.

"Shad," Shadrack announced firmly.

"Wh-what, sir?"

"Everyone in town calls me Shad. They won't know who

you're talking about if you address me otherwise." He peeled off his work apron and hung it on its peg against the back wall. His favorite black beret followed. A quick perusal of the tidy work area behind the counter ensured him everything was where it belonged and ready for their first stream of morning customers. The oak countertop was free of dust and clutter. Yesterday's messages were carefully filed away, other than the few that still needed to be delivered. The printer was loaded with paper, and the waiting area on the other side of the counter was freshly mopped. The sun was spilling welcome shoots of light through the wide picture window overlooking the plank floor where their customers would soon line up.

Bram shifted from one boot to the other, ran a hand up the black suspender riding his injured left shoulder, and tugged at the front of his white collar with one finger. "What I mean, sir, are you certain it's wise to leave me alone on my first day of work?"

For an answer, Shad reached for one of his spare pens and sent it sailing in an arc across the work area.

On reflex, Bram released his hold on his collar and caught the pen in mid-air.

Shad hid a grin. He harbored no doubts whatsoever about the lad's suitability for his new job. Though his impressive height required him to stoop over the telegraph machine, he'd flawlessly sent a half dozen test messages last night and this morning already. He'd proven to be a natural at calibrating and tinkering with the machine. Shad could hardly believe his luck in finding such a bright and promising candidate to bring on board. His superiors at the federal marshal's office in Tucson were going to be delighted to hear about his own newly freed-up work schedule. They needed him in the field on their latest case, not perched atop a telegraph machine.

"You'll soon discover I only make decisions I'm certain about." *Ninety-nine percent of the time, at least...* He hoped the letter he'd written to the Boomtown Mail Order Brides Company a few weeks ago would not prove to be an exception to that rule. A quick glance at his watch showed he had less than an hour to change clothes and get himself to the train station.

"All the same, sir." Bram realigned his perfectly stacked sheaf of papers on the countertop and nudged his ink jar a smidgen to the right. "I'd prefer to have you hovering in the background for a few minutes after we open for business."

"Can't." Shad paused with his hand on the doorknob of the stairway leading to his second story loft apartment. "I'm getting married this morning."

It was a decision he'd made after the same careful information gathering and planning in which he approached every other facet of his life. His instincts as an undercover investigator had demanded it.

Bram's jolt of surprise knocked his stack of papers sideways. He quickly returned them to their perfect sentinel alignment. "Married, sir?"

Shad nodded. "In comparison, I imagine sending a few telegrams will seem…" He paused to let his words sink in.

"Like a Sunday morning stroll, sir?" Bram's tone was half-questioning, half-rueful.

"Shad," he corrected. "If possible, I'll return around noon to check on your status and answer any questions, but I won't be able to stay long." He planned to do something he rarely did — spend an afternoon at his ranch. It would give him the opportunity to introduce his new bride to his staff and help her settle in, not that he expected her to be traveling with much luggage.

He made his exit before his new employee could voice any more first-day jitters. Jogging two stairs at a time, he ascended to the humble loft where he'd spent way too many lonely nights. The long hours he worked between his two jobs made the commute to his ranch on the north side of town difficult during the week, so he'd fallen into the habit of bunking at the office. It was a habit that would have to change with the acquisition of a new wife. And the family he hoped to raise with her, Lord willing...

He peered into the oval mirror hanging over his basin and grimaced at his un-groom-like appearance. The slouching, boyish clerk he pretended to be stared back at him. Since he was an average looking man who possessed an average build and average height, he'd always found it easy to transform himself into any role his job required him to play. With just the right wig and suit jacket and just the right amount of face paint, he could age himself twenty years or more in two snaps.

The fake smattering of freckles he'd painted on earlier were the first items to go. It was only fair for his new bride to see the real Shad Nicholson. A woman deserved to know exactly whom she was marrying, at least as far as appearances went. There were things he wasn't at liberty to share with her about his job — his *real* job as a federal marshal. The truth was, he might not ever be at liberty to share such things with her.

It was one of the many reasons he'd chosen to marry a bride via the mail. Not only did the process avoid the exhaustive perils of courting, he imagined most women resorting to such a nontraditional mode of marriage came from humble, impoverished backgrounds. In short, it was his hope Miss Gladstone would be too grateful to him for rescuing her from a life of penny-pinching to question his long absences from home.

His mop of sandy-brown curls and sideburns were the next things to go. He swiftly clipped them away, revealing the darker, auburn hued hair beneath. With his hair shorter, he looked much more like the twenty-six years he actually was. Instead of donning his Sunday-best suit like most normal men would have, he opted to dress the part of a gentleman rancher. Perhaps he was still playing a role, but he wanted Miss Gladstone to be very much aware she was marrying a cowboy.

He tucked a snowy white dress shirt into black trousers and stepped into a pair of boots shined to black glass. Next, he shrugged into a brown leather vest and affixed a bolo around his collar. It was held in place by a silver disc bearing a five-pointed star, a tongue-in-cheek nod to his status as a federal agent.

Shad had to walk two blocks to reach the stable where he boarded his team of horses and parked his curricle. It was a sleek, black metal rig with a wide sun canopy stretched over a padded seat of ivory leather. The Headstone Train Depot itself was a good mile away on the south side of town, and it was slow going for a pair of horses and a buggy on the crowded streets. By the time he drew abreast of the arrival platform, it was blasting its horns and easing into the station. *Perfect timing!*

Other carriages and wagons nosed their way around him on all sides, temporarily hemming him in. Disembarking passengers flooded the platform like ants. Some threw themselves into the arms of loved ones, while others hurried to the hovering collection of wagons. The rest of them spilled down the stairs and scattered down the perfectly woven north, south, east and west streets of the city.

Soon, only a small collection of carriages remained. He murmured to his team of prancing Missouri Fox Trotters to urge them forward to fill in the gap left by the last departing wagon, putting him at the center of the stairs. He'd special ordered the pair of black stallions from a breeder in the midwest. Their unique four-beat gait had served him well while hitched to various rigs and also when he needed to make speed across the desert while in the saddle. His horse handler at the ranch was busy procuring another pair, so he could begin breeding his own herd.

He scanned the near-empty train platform, trying to catch sight of any woman who matched the description Miss Gladstone had included in her letter. She'd mentioned blonde hair and claimed she would be wearing a brown gown, but he could see no one so simply dressed, unless... His jaw dropped at the beauty with long, corkscrew curls. She was standing beside a growing mountain of luggage, smiling merrily at the various attendants unloading her things from the train and directing them where to stack each item.

He supposed, by some stretch, her gown could be called brown, but that was a gargantuan understatement. It was a rich coffee-colored brocade edged with lavish puffs of ivory lace at the neckline and sleeves. A burgundy silk bodice and underskirt peeped from yet more layers of lace. He was skilled at profiling suspects, and his well-trained eyes told him the gown was custom made and cost a fortune.

The first trickle of alarm worked its way down his spine as he leaped down from his rig, steadied his horses, and walked around to the passenger side. A myriad of theories burst across his investigator's mind. Perhaps his letter had been intercepted by an enemy, and she'd been sent as a double agent to undermine his work. Or perhaps some wealthy young debutante had thought the whole mail-order bride process sounded like a good lark. Perhaps...

The stunning woman raised her warm hazel gaze to his, and all other suppositions flew from his brain. "Mr. Nicholson?" she trilled in a low, musical alto. As regal as a princess, she glided with cultured ease down the stairs in his direction.

For a moment, all he could do was nod and accept her outstretched, white-gloved hands. Even in high-heeled boots, she was a few inches shorter than him, forcing her to tip her oval face up to his.

"I'm Meg. Your affianced." A faint blush stained her high cheeks and forehead.

After a pause, he recovered his power of speech. "It's a pleasure to finally meet you." He raised her hands to brush his mouth over her knuckles. She'd sounded intelligent and engaging in her letters, but her correspondence had in no way prepared him to face a rare beauty like this. She possessed the classical kind of features that inspired verses to be written and portraits to be commissioned — wide, expressive eyes; a perfect curve to her swan-like neck; and white, even teeth when she smiled.

"Likewise." As she watched him from beneath half-closed lids with curiosity and no small amount of shrewd speculation, it dawned on him she was not the quiet, demure wife he'd been expecting. It was also clear she was not the least bit impoverished, which begged one very important question.

"Why?" he asked softly, lowering her hands though he kept his loosely clasped around hers.

She smiled impishly up at him, not bothering to make any coy attempts at misunderstanding. "I could ask you the same, sir."

"Shad," he insisted, suddenly and inexplicably wanting to hear his name uttered in her delicious voice. Years of solitude and loneliness fled in the face of so much loveliness.

"Very well, Shad." He instantly adored the way her carefully modulated voice turned his simple nickname to music. "Why did you send for me?"

He opened and shut his mouth. Every reason he'd ordered a bride now seemed grossly presumptuous, not to mention desperately prideful. He'd hoped for a quiet, dutiful woman who wouldn't question his strange schedule, long work hours, and frequent absences. He'd expected a woman much plainer in appearance and much needier in her finances, one who would be wildly grateful to him for every dollar he handed her. He'd dreamed of a wife who'd assume the reins of his household staff with quiet efficiency, one who would also birth and rear his children and fill his silent home with laughter and happy voices. What a fool he'd been to think he could turn his daydreams into reality with the penning of a single letter to some matchmaking agency in Boston!

And how in tarnation had the Bransons ever thought Margaret Vivienne Gladstone was the strong, resilient woman he'd so meticulously described in his letter? She resembled a china doll that a strong wind would blow into the next town over. He knew without peeling her silk gloves from her delicate fingers that her hands had never milked a cow or gathered chicken eggs. Every detail about her appearance screamed she was pampered and soft.

At his silence, she let out a soft, breathy sigh, and some of the expectant light dimmed in her eyes. "You're disappointed in who they sent you." She tried to withdraw her fingers from his, but his hands tightened around hers on their own accord.

"No, I..." He glanced away from her mildly accusing expression while guilt flooded his chest. "You're quite simply..." He returned his gaze to hers, determined to see this conversation through. He owed her that. "Not what I expected. Much lovelier, in fact." *So stunning you take the air right out of my lungs.*

To his consternation, the sparkle finished disappearing from her eyes. "Useless, you mean." She gave his hands a light yank, and her lips twisted bitterly. "A frivolous ornament to be set on a shelf and admired, not a woman capable of taking life by the horns and holding her own. If you think I've not been accused of that before, you're sorely mistaken."

Her vehemence caught him off guard, and more guilt infused him at the knowledge she'd pegged his assessment of her with all too deadly accuracy. He was drowning in remorse yet did not know what to say to make things right with her.

"Do you wish to terminate our contract?" she inquired, holding his gaze steadily. There were no tears or vapors; every word was spoken quietly and without emotion. "I've certainly no intention of holding you to a union you do not want."

Her bitter question shook him from his reverie like a splash of cold spring water. "Good heavens, no!" he exploded.

She looked surprised, and the tinge of pink in her cheeks deepened. "Oh, this is awkward," she moaned softly.

"It is," he agreed. A shame-faced grin tugged at his lips. Ah, but they'd gotten off to a rough start, and it was entirely his own fault. Only a rattle-brained idiot would send this gorgeous woman back to Boston on the next train for the infraction of failing to be poor and plain. By all that was holy, he was a man of his word. That was a fact that never altered, no matter which role he happened to be playing. If that entailed marrying a slightly spoiled, overly indulged princess in this particular instance, then so be it.

A chuckle escaped her. "You're not what I expected, either," she confessed. A bit of the sparkle returned to her eyes.

"Oh?" It was impossible not to share in her ill-concealed merriment. Her laugh was so vibrant and alive it pulled a fellow right in.

She tossed her head, making her corkscrew curls bounce and slide across her perfectly rounded shoulders. "It is the wild west after all. You were supposed to be sunburnt, dusty, and twirling no less than two pistols as you strode in my direction."

This time, his wry chuckle mingled with hers. *Ah, but you're as green as they come, lass.* "I am sorry to disappoint, ma'am." Unlike the cowpokes skidding across the desert on their half-wild mustangs, he generally kept his weapons out of sight. He had a pistol strapped beneath his vest, a second one tucked in the back waistband of his trousers, and a blade sheathed inside each boot. Such was his life — real weapons, real danger. Good gravy, but he had no business bringing an innocent young debutante into the mix. Man of his word or not, the right thing would be to put her on the next train, to send her back to the world of dances, tea parties, and charity luncheons where she belonged.

Alas, the dark and selfish side of him wasn't near ready to give her up. She was like sunshine on legs, spilling light with every word she spoke and every step she took.

Another short, melodious laugh escaped her. "I do not recall stating I was disappointed."

His heart skipped at least three beats, and the merriment between them disappeared. It was replaced by something far more tense, more potent.

He brushed the pads of his thumbs over the tops of her hands and heard himself saying. "I am very glad to hear it, Meg, because I wish to marry you. This morning, if you're willing." *Before I come to my senses and change my mind.*

Unless a lightning bolt zapped him from above for ignoring his better judgement, so help him. He was going through with this union!

CHAPTER 3: SHOTGUN WEDDING

"Now?" Meg squeaked. Her female brain quaked at the thought of how many travel creases must be in her gown, and how many hairs were surely out of place after a full week aboard the train. Her private travel car had contained every creature comfort possible, but it wasn't the same as donning a wedding gown in a proper dressing room surrounded by mirrors, jewelry boxes, powders, and perfumes. She tried not to think about the bevy of maids and attendants she'd left behind. That part of her life was over, though it would have been nice to enjoy a wee bit of assistance on a special occasion like today.

Shad's jaw tightened, and his brown gaze took on a shuttered cast that made her wonder if he was having second thoughts. She was normally an excellent interpreter of body language, but this particular man was turning out to be difficult to read.

"Please forgive me if I've made any false assumptions about your situation, ma'am. If you'd prefer to postpone the ceremony until your family and friends can travel to town—"

"That will not be necessary," she interjected quickly. The

only family she had left were a few distant cousins in London whom she'd not had the pleasure of meeting. "I was merely hoping to freshen up and change first." That was only partly true. She honestly hadn't considered the possibility her intended might expect her to join him in holy matrimony the moment she stepped off the train. Her head was spinning at the notion, but stalling would only give him time to reconsider. He clearly did not believe she was cut out for life in the west now that he'd gotten an eyeful of her expensive gown. It was a dead shame, because she very much liked what she saw in him.

"Of course." Her affianced lifted her into his curricle as if she weighed no more than a bird feather. "You may have all the time you wish to dress. I've arranged for the minister to conduct a private ceremony at my ranch. Sheriff Otera and Judge Spolidora will be attending as our witnesses."

She studied him from beneath her lashes. A sheriff and a judge were interesting friends for a mere telegraph clerk to possess. Perhaps their social connection was more due to his status as a gentleman rancher.

"It sounds as if you've thought of everything," she murmured. Shad Nicholson was turning out to be exactly the man she'd painted in her picture of a perfect life. He was neither the tallest nor the handsomest man she'd ever met, but he was well-mannered and kind, a perfect gentleman right down to his faint British accent. Most importantly, he'd chosen her from whatever lineup of candidates Mr. Branson had sent him from the Boomtown Mail Order Brides Company — her! The *real* her. Not some wealthy heiress, because she'd given strict orders to withhold that detail from the application process.

"Not quite everything." Shad's tone was dry as he nodded at her mountainous pile of luggage. "Pardon me a moment." He strode up the stairs to address the army of attendants who were still unloading her train car. She watched him gesture with both hands as if giving directions. Then he produced a wad of money and doled out several bills. Moments later, the attendants began to load her belongings inside a trio of wagons parked on the east side of the platform.

He returned and climbed into the driver's seat of the curricle beside her.

"Thank you," she murmured, grateful for his assistance with her belongings. In addition to his growing list of attributes, it appeared he was also a generous man. He hadn't hesitated to spend his own funds to ensure her property was properly transported.

"You're my family now, and family takes care of family." Without looking up at her, he yanked lightly on the reins to get his horses trotting.

Family. His words soared to the emptiest crevices in her heart and nestled there. "I've always wanted a family." She spoke the words so softly she wasn't certain he heard them.

"So have I." He continued to stare straight ahead as the horses plodded down the hard-packed clay city streets, past sun-bleached storefronts and dusty saloon porches with weathered gray planks. "Jordan Branson informed me you recently lost a parent. I am sorry to hear it. This must be a difficult time for you."

She shrugged. "It was nearly a year ago. We weren't close."

Shad's brows rose, and she hastened to explain. "He was a good man, and he loved me in his own way." He'd been stern and distant, not one to spare even the smallest gesture of affection, such as a hair ruffle or a cuff on the shoulder. "It's just that he was gone most of the time. The truth is, I was raised by nurses and nannies." Whom he'd fired on a regular basis for the smallest of infractions… There were also unsmiling housekeepers, jumpy-as-a-wildcat grooms and riding instructors, and scads of be-spectacled women determined to instill in her every last social grace. There'd been dance instructors, deportment coaches, and French tutors. The only lessons she'd truly enjoyed were the ones involving painting and sculpting.

"And your mother?" Shad's expression was unreadable as he exchanged a quick, sideways glance with her.

"She passed when I was a wee child. I have no memory of her." Only a single, beautiful portrait she'd spent hours of her childhood staring at, trying to conjure up some faint snatch of memory. "What about you?" She strove to lay aside her sadness by forcing a teasing note into her voice. "Will I inherit any dragon family members with ferocious ideas about daughters-in-law I cannot possibly hope to measure up to?"

He gave a bark of laughter that sounded a bit on the rusty side. Something told her he wasn't a man accustomed to laughing much. "No. I was orphaned at a young age and raised by an aging uncle who is no longer with us. Alas, there are no fire-breathing dragons on my ranch. Nothing but ordinary horses, cows, hens, a pack of dogs, and one very snooty cat the sharecroppers' children named Miss Hiss."

O-o-o-h-h-h! He owned dogs *and* a cat. How utterly marvelous! Her father had never allowed either in their Boston townhome or country estate. He'd insisted she focus on her studies in deportment without interruption from "some slobbering mutt."

The bustling town of Headstone disappeared and was replaced by a sandy stretch of mesas and canyons. Beyond that were scattered grasslands punctuated by clusters of Joshua trees and cacti. At last, Shad's ranch popped into view.

It so closely resembled her painting of her perfect life that she stared in stunned silence. A long, circle drive led to a rambling two-story with a wide wrap-around porch. The exterior was made of beige stucco and boasted a red tile roof with three chimneys. Beyond the home, a red clay path extended to a collection of barns and outbuildings, pastures, and peacefully grazing beasts.

Shad brought his team of horses to a stop at the front door of the farmhouse. A young Hispanic groom hurried to grab the reins. *"Hola, Señor* Shad. Welcome home!" He wore dusty boots, faded overalls over a plaid shirt, and a grin stretching from one side of his coppery, sun-kissed face to the other.

"Thank you, Carlo. This is my bride-to-be, Meg Gladstone."

He offered her a bashful smile brimming with curiosity. *"Hola, Señorita."*

"Meg," she corrected gently as Shad handed her down from the curricle.

"Yes'm, Miss Meg," he answered politely and continued to ogle her with uncloaked admiration until Shad cleared his throat.

"I'll get these horses put up," he muttered, leaping into the driver's seat. With a tip of his straw hat, he set off in the direction of the nearest outbuilding.

Shad didn't immediately step away from her as they surveyed his home together. "I don't suppose it looks much like what you're accustomed to," he noted dryly.

She made a sniffing sound. What an understatement! "Not even close. I was raised in a palatial fortress surrounded by platoons of servants." She didn't miss her old life one bit.

"I see." He sounded grim.

She glanced up at him. "I don't believe you do. This..." She waved her hands in delight to take in the rustic scene. "This is so much better."

"Oh?" He arched a brow at her, searching her features.

"You've made a home here, Shad. A real home." She gave a small squeal as she caught sight of a calico slinking around the porch bannister railing to get a better look at her. "One with a cat. Oh, you darling, darling creature!"

"Careful, Meg!"

Shad's warning was lost on her as she left his side to approach the bristling feline. "I hear you're a difficult little thing, Miss Hiss." She slowly reached out a gloved hand, careful not to make any quick, jerky movements that might startle her. "But I'm not one to swallow gossip without a second thought. No, indeed. Something tells me there's more to you than meets the eye, little one." She understood all too well what it felt like to be labeled and judged without a chance to defend oneself.

The cat reared back and hissed at her, but she otherwise held her ground, staring suspiciously as Meg crept closer. After a pregnant pause, she jutted her furry snout forward to sniff hesitantly at her hand. Then, without any further preamble, she ducked her head and butted it against her palm.

"I cannot believe what I'm seeing," Shad muttered. "That cat won't go to anyone. The only reason I keep her around is to thin the herd of vermin."

Meg nickered softly at the cat and smoothed her silky head. "Maybe if you showed her a little more appreciation, she'd let you pet her as well."

As if understanding her words, Miss Hiss began to purr. It wasn't a muted kitten purr, either. It was a loud rumble that made Shad chuckle.

"Well, that's a menacing sound if I ever heard one."

Meg rolled her eyes at Miss Hiss. "See? No appreciation. But that's quite alright, since we ladies are going to stick together from now on, eh?"

Miss Hiss purred louder and butted her head against Meg's hand again.

It was with great reluctance that Meg stood and faced her intended groom once more. "I should order a bath before our guests start to arrive. How long before my trunks are delivered?"

"Within the hour, I hope." He looked amused. "I may not possess a platoon of servants, but my housekeeper, Valentina, will be delighted to help you unpack. Which of your dozens of trunks should I have her dive into first?"

"The largest one," she supplied breezily, ignoring the dig at her exorbitant amount of luggage. "It contains my wedding dress."

"Your wedding dress," Shad repeated carefully, as if doubting he heard correctly.

"Yes, indeed. I had it designed in New York City by one of the finest tailors on the east coast. I wasn't certain if there would be a dressmaker in Arizona up to the task." Nor had she anticipated marrying so quickly. It was a good thing she'd come prepared.

Two hours later, she stood next to her groom before a minister holding a large, leather-bound Bible. Behind him rose a wide stone fireplace. To their right stood Judge Spolidora in his black overcoat and top hat, leaning heavily on a cane. At his side was the town sheriff, Chase Otera. His silver star caught the flickering light from the hearth, emitting a fiery twinkle.

"Dearly beloved," the minister intoned. "We gather together today…"

Meg was drenched in a gown of white lace with a train that extended a good six feet behind her. It had taken

Valentina no less than ten full minutes to connect all the seed pearl buttons running down her shoulder blades to her lower back. The starry-eyed woman had sighed over and over again at what a vision she was in her dress.

The short ceremony passed in a blur for Meg. She could barely focus on the words and mumbled, "I do," when prompted. *I'm getting married. I'm actually getting married!* Things were happening so quickly her brain couldn't quite comprehend it all.

"I now pronounce you husband and wife," their minister concluded. "You may seal this holy union with a kiss."

A kiss! Meg lifted her startled gaze to Shad's, swamped with a dozen conflicting, indescribable feelings. If only she'd a mother to advise her or a female friend to confide in. Alas, she possessed no one to help prepare her for this moment.

Her new husband was studying her with a heavy lidded expression. The black suit and white shirt he'd changed into for their wedding had transformed him from a simple cowboy into something more lordly. In that moment, she knew with certainty he could have held his own on any dance floor in Boston or New York. His face was clean shaven, but there was a roguish hint of an afternoon shadow riding his upper lip and jaw. He offered her a half-smile that for some reason gave her heart an unsettling tug.

Then, in slow motion, he cupped her face with long, steady fingers and leaned down to brush his mouth against hers.

It was as if his very soul reached out to embrace her.

Meg caught her breath at the wonder of it. Her lips trembled beneath his, and an extraordinary warmth stole through her. To be so cherished by another person was something she'd dreamt of a thousand times, never quite believing it would ever happen to her. She barely knew this man, yet already she was beginning to trust him. Given enough time, she might even come to feel affection for him.

Contentment washed in slow, soothing waves across the storm of her uncertainty. It appeared the Lord had seen fit to provide her with a good man despite her somewhat scandalous method of seeking out a husband. Her fearful gamble had paid off. She wouldn't have stood half a chance of procuring such honesty in a union back east — not with her fortune and reputation eclipsing the real woman beneath.

Shad studied her for several long moments before dropping his hands and taking a half step back. Even then, he continued to regard her with a slightly dazed expression that made her wonder if he'd felt the same things she'd felt when he kissed her — the soul-shaking connection and the staggering warmth that had accompanied it.

There were papers to sign and the judge and sheriff's hands to shake. Meg felt like she was seeing the world through a thick morning haze and nearly forgot about the documents her attorney had given her to travel with. Only when the judge was saying his goodbyes did she remember.

"Wait, please," she declared softly. "It is probably best if you take a look at my father's last will and testament before you depart. My attorney tried to explain it, but all I can recall is my future husband and his solicitor will be required to manage some accounts for me."

Her travel trunks were crammed inside the entry foyer, stacked end to end against the wall. Shad followed her wordlessly as she pointed out the one containing the documents in question. He returned with her to the living room, silently scanning them.

Whatever he read made his face turn a bright red. Unless she was mistaken, he looked both horrified and angry as he handed the documents over to the judge.

"Now what?" she pleaded softly.

He rounded on her, jaw clenched grimly. "You're worth a king's fortune, that's what!"

"Yes." She scowled at him, despising with all her energy how quickly her money always seemed to ruin things for her. "Is that going to be a problem for us?" *Please say no. I'm begging you!* For the first time since she said *I do*, she felt like weeping. She'd traveled so far and come so close to her first taste of true happiness.

He scanned her face as if seeing her for the first time. "You knew what you were worth, yet you chose to travel all the way from Boston…alone?"

Her eyes widened at the horrified tremor in his voice. "Yes."

"You should have had an escort by your side at all times," he ground out. "Someone to protect you. Preferably a bunch of someones to protect you!"

She dropped her gaze, no longer able to bear the angry, accusing simmer in his coffee brew eyes. She hardly recognized the man who'd kissed her so tenderly a few minutes earlier. "I thought I was escaping all that by coming here. I am desperately weary of being kept under lock and key." She had no intention of going back to the life her father had forced her to live beneath his iron thumbs. She had no intention of spending the rest of her days cowering behind servants and bodyguards. Now that she'd tasted freedom, she was certain she could never again live without it.

Shad let out a low groan and briefly closed his eyes. "Surely you understand that hopping a train out west did not suddenly lower your net worth."

"Of course I know that!" She was exasperated at his tone and wondered where this line of questioning was leading. *Good gracious!* If the wild west wasn't far enough to outrun her father's King Midas legacy, then she was ready to give away every last penny of it. Which she most unfortunately did not have the legal authority to do…

His eyelids snapped open. "Then you had to have also known the risks you were taking by traveling alone. I may never sleep another wink just thinking about all the things that could have gone wrong."

"Such as…" she taunted, thoroughly incensed by his attitude. Their ultra short acquaintance hardly justified such a vehement reaction from him.

"Kidnapping and ransom come to mind," he shot back.

No! Her blood chilled a few degrees in her veins. He was wrong. Her father was dead and his business interests transferred to someone besides herself. She'd been very careful. That part of her life was over, and she didn't miss it one bit.

They glared at each other for an extended, heated moment. It gradually dawned on her that her new husband was truly fearful on her behalf. He'd not said one blessed word of thanks to her for transforming him into a man of vast wealth; all he'd done so far was harp about her safety.

She breathed through her indignation, relaxing in slow degrees. Perhaps God had sent her across the country to just the right man after all. "Well, I have you to protect me now," she announced mildly, once she was calm enough to speak again. "You swore it to me in your vows. I have witnesses," she teased, stepping closer to him.

His hands gripped her upper arms as if he wanted to shake her. He leaned in to speak in a tight voice against her temple. "You could have at least warned me, Meg."

"Perhaps I did not wish to scare you away." Her tone was rollicking.

"I do not scare easily," he retorted roughly. "But this?" He drew back a few inches. "This scares me, Meg. Only a fool would feel otherwise."

"Pshaw! I am no longer connected in any way to Gladstone Trans-Atlantic Shipping. My attorney saw to it that every tie between us was severed."

His hands tightened on her arms. "It doesn't alter the fact you are one of the wealthiest women on the continent."

The coldness returned to her veins, making her shiver. "No one besides you needs to know. I am married and have a new name. My old life is over," she insisted.

"Is it?" His gaze burned into hers. "Marriages are a matter of public record. What's to keep an unscrupulous person from your past from threatening your safety to gain access to the vast funds I now manage?"

She shivered. "You, I suppose?"

"Yes. Me." His voice was bleak.

CHAPTER 4: MARITAL WOES

Meg refused to let Shad's unsubstantiated fears disturb her calm. A person could not sit around and fret over every shadow their imagination could conjure up. If any real threats to her safety manifested themselves, she would worry about them at that time and not a moment sooner.

She was too busy enjoying her new life to wallow in needless worry; and by the end of her first day at her husband's ranch, she was completely in love with his farmhouse. Unlike the stately mansions where she'd previously lived with their perfectly symmetrical balconies, cupolas, and pillars, this home had been added to a dozen or more times by the previous owners, giving a person the impression that it rambled on and on forever.

It was spacious and full of light, thanks to the many oversized windows dotting the walls. The four main rooms in the center of the home — the kitchen, family room, parlor, and entry foyer that contained the stairwell leading to the second story — were actually built of logs. They'd long since been covered by planks and stucco, but Meg found the extra deep windowsills to be a charming feature. She could imagine her sculpting projects on display there.

On the east side of the home, an enormous sunken living room had been added that was large enough to host any number of dances and parties. She decided on the spot the oversized portrait of her mother would grace one of these walls.

To the west, a dining room had been added on to the kitchen, and a master bedchamber and water closet with plumbing and running water had been added beyond the parlor. Meg blushed at the thought of sharing the suite with her new husband. Would he expect her to sleep there with him tonight, or would he wait to pursue the more intimate side of their marital relationship once they had the opportunity to become better acquainted?

She stood in the doorway of the bedchamber, holding up her left hand to gaze at the enormous opal Shad had placed on her ring finger during their wedding ceremony. It was surrounded by tiny diamonds in an antique gold setting. It was so lovely she could stare at it the rest of the day without getting her fill of it. Her imagination conjured up one story after another, each one more fantastic than the last, about where it had come from. It was old and of heirloom quality, so it was highly likely it had been worn by another bride before her.

"Do you like it?" Her husband's voice wafted over her from behind.

She spun around so quickly she nearly tripped on the train of her wedding gown.

He'd been hefting one of her many trunks into the room, but he hastily set down his burden to help her catch her equilibrium. His suit jacket was missing, and his white shirtsleeves were rolled, exposing tanned forearms.

"I do," she confessed breathlessly. "It is a beautiful ring. I thank you for it."

"I wasn't certain how you would feel about wearing something so old."

After you met me and realized how wealthy I am. Her brain filled in what he left unsaid. She searched for the right words to set his mind at ease. "I like that it has a history, that it once belonged to someone in your family, and the sense of... connection it gives me." She'd been alone for so long that even a small and distant connection meant something to her.

"It belonged to my great-aunt once upon a time." His mouth twisted. "Or so I've been told. It was given to me by my great-uncle's solicitor after he passed."

"The one who raised you?" she asked curiously.

"Yes."

Shad gave a muffled grunt as he picked up her truck and carried it the rest of the way into the room. "To be honest, I never met her. The ship that brought my parents and me from London sank a few miles off the coast. I was rounded up with the rest of the surviving children and sent to an orphanage in Boston. It was six years before my great uncle found me there. By then, his wife had passed."

He and his family were immigrants? Meg studied her new husband's profile as he added the trunk he carried to the growing stack against the far wall. That certainly explained his British accent. It also explained why he was alone in the world. What a horrible way to lose one's parents and at such a young age, too! Her heart ached at the thought of him spending six long years in an orphanage, grieving and wondering what would become of him. She could only imagine the terrors and uncertainties he'd endured.

Meg knew a thing or two about orphanages from the many charity events she'd attended, enough to realize he'd likely known cold and hunger during his stay there. She wanted to weep for all he'd suffered. Instead, she strove again to find the right words. "Though you never met your aunt, she was still family. I'll always have the pleasure of knowing I am wearing a ring that once belonged to her."

Shad shook his head, but he did not appear displeased. "Aren't you a fanciful creature?"

"A romantic at heart, yes. I suppose it's the artist in me." She caught sight of Valentina hovering just outside the doorway. "There you are, my dear. Help me out of these endless rows of buttons once more, and I'll be forever in your debt."

"Yes, ma'am!" Valentina sailed into the room, smoothing her crisp white apron as she walked. She turned impulsively to her employer. "Isn't your bride a vision in so much lace, *Señor* Shad?"

He straightened and met Meg's gaze. For several moments, they were lost in each other's eyes. "Yes," he confessed at last. "She is enchanting."

Meg suddenly wished the two of them were alone in the room. She wanted to finish drowning in his eyes. She wanted to feel his lips on hers again. She wanted...

"Pardon me." Shad bolted from the room so quickly her head spun.

She stared after him.

"He is quite taken with you," Valentina sighed with a hand to her heart. She was an attractive Hispanic woman in her late thirties or early forties with a cascade of dark, wavy hair and a quick smile.

If only I could believe you! Meg swallowed a sigh, knowing her husband was still coming to terms with the fact he'd been saddled with a wife he considered to be a frivolous socialite.

The housekeeper shut the bedchamber door and went to work on her seed pearl buttons. She chattered incessantly as she nimbly undid each button. "We are so happy *Señor* Shad has finally taken a wife. A home this size needs more than a handful of dogs and a cat. It needs a woman's touch, children, and laughter."

Meg blushed at the notion of bearing Shad children and hastily changed the subject. "How long have you worked for him?"

"Nigh on three years, *bella*. It is a good job, the best job I've ever had. *Señor* is a kind and generous employer."

A fact that surprised Meg not one whit.

"Though he is gone entirely too much, if you ask me," Valentina added with asperity. "I hope he will cease working such long hours now that he has a wife."

Meg peeled off her gloves and tossed them on a nearby dresser. "I never imagined how long and hard a telegraph operator would be required to work."

The housekeeper made a harrumphing sound of disapproval and did not immediately reply.

"It seems to me the town could justify hiring him an assistant or even a second operator if the workload is so demanding."

"He took on an apprentice over the weekend," Valentina offered. "But between you and me, *chica*, I'm not certain how much time this lad is going to save him. Bram Fairfield is one of the miners' sons. He'll have much to learn, which I fear will take even more of your husband's time."

Meg knew it was way too soon to mention it, but there was another possibility altogether. Now that Shad Nicholson was married to her, he could quit his job at the telegraph office altogether. With the money she'd brought into their marriage, he would never have to work another day of his life.

Until he reached that happy conclusion for himself, however, she would strive to make his home at the ranch his private oasis. She would fill it with art, music, freshly washed and press bed linens, and the heavenly scents of home-cooked meals — not that she'd prepared a single meal in her life, but she would learn.

"Who does the cooking around here?" she demanded. Her mind was already racing ahead to the recipes she would try out on her groom.

"Tandy Holmes. She's our cook." Valentina sniffed. "She puts on airs sometimes, because of that attorney downtown who's her cousin, but she makes tolerable enough food."

Oh, dear! Tolerable would never do. Meg wanted so much better than tolerable for her wonderful new husband. Her mind raced ahead to all the spectacular entrees she would prepare for him. After a lifetime of enjoying the masterpieces of the most skilled culinary artists in the east, she knew what she was talking about.

It looked as if she and Tolerable Tandy had a bit of learning to do together. Yes, indeed. She would have that all-important talk with her cook today. Her mind made up, she changed into a gown of burgundy silk. There was nothing like a fresh gown and hair style to prepare a woman for a coming tête-à-tête.

But first, she and Valentina tackled the long and arduous task of unpacking. Only a few minutes into the task, it became clear they were desperately short of wardrobe space for her many gowns, cloaks, riding habits, hats, boots, and shoes.

"Well!" Meg plopped down on Shad's four-poster bed with a bounce of sheer perplexity. Not only was she short of hanging space, there wasn't room to move more than one or two more wardrobes into the cozy bedchamber. That was a problem, because she needed a good six more, maybe ten!

"You'd think with as many times as the last owners added on to this house they'd have included a dressing room," she sighed.

Wait! That was it! She gazed around the master suite in

speculation. Shad's bed anchored the small space with a simple navy quilt. On the far wall was a stone fireplace. To her left was a dresser with a mirror, and beside it a small desk. To her right was the pair of wardrobes she was having difficulty fitting her things into.

"We should push out the whole wall, fireplace and all," she mused. That would give her plenty of new space to work with.

Valentina gasped. "Why, that would cost a fortune!"

Which I have, though I do not believe it will cost nearly that much, my dear woman. She stood, anxious to get started. "Who should I speak to about this?"

"Your husband, of course." The housekeeper looked puzzled.

Bah! She couldn't imagine him raising any objections to such a small and practical project. Her mind leaped ahead to what needed to happen next. "And who would he normally call on to handle a job like this?"

"My own husband, I suppose." But the woman looked doubtful. "It seems an awful lot of trouble to go through to make room for a few more dresses, *bella*."

Meg muffled a snort. She had at least three dozen more gowns waiting to be unpacked and that didn't begin to account for all her accessories, petticoats, and other things. She gave a decided nod. "Have your husband report to me after dinner."

Valentina inclined her head. "As you wish, *Señora*."

"In the meantime, I'll finish my tour of the house. Then I will assist Tandy with getting dinner started."

Valentina looked horrified. "Nobody messes in the kitchen without Tandy's permission, *Señora*."

Meg stiffened, knowing her father would have never tolerated such insubordination. She drew herself up to her full height, which she valiantly wished was a few inches taller. "To begin with, I am not a nobody. I'm the new mistress of this home. Do you understand, Valentina?"

The woman looked horrified. "*Sí, señora.* I know your place and mine. I truly do. It's just that—"

Meg stopped her defensive babble with an upraised hand. "Secondly, I do not make a habit of creating messes in the kitchen or any other room in the house. I intend to cook." Or rather, she intended to learn to cook. Surely such an endeavor wouldn't prove too difficult for a woman with her fine palate and vast dining experience.

"*Sí, señora.*" Valentina sounded close to tears. "I will inform Tandy you wish to pay her a visit."

"You'll do nothing of the sort!" Meg was aghast. "I will come and go as I please in my own home."

"*Sí, señora.*" Her housekeeper dashed the backs of her hands across her eyes, leaving her utterly mystified as to what she had said or done that was so upsetting to the woman.

Her cheerful chatter was entirely extinguished. She escorted her mistress upstairs in complete silence, only speaking once they reached the second floor. "There are guest rooms on both sides of the stairs and a water closet in between."

"What about that door?" Meg pointed at the shorter-than-average wood paneled door at the top of the landing. It was barely tall enough for her to pass through; Shad would have to stoop to enter it.

"It leads to the attic, *señora.*"

"Meg," she corrected absently. "My name is Meg."

"*Sí, Señora* Meg."

She sighed at the woman's persistence in maintaining formalities between them and reached for the door handle, half expecting more objections. Valentina merely clamped her lips shut.

They mounted the attic stairs, Meg in front and Valentina following closely behind her. Stifling a sneeze from all the dust, she gazed at the short, cathedral ceiling at the top of the stairs. The room had promise.

It was long and narrow due to the pitch of the roof, which fell to about four feet on each side. A pair of dormer windows, one facing the front of the home and the other facing the rear, helped open the space somewhat. A thin assortment of boxes and trunks littered the floor space. Most importantly, it looked unused. She'd not be tromping on anyone else's turf by claiming the space as her own.

"This will be perfect for my studio." Meg spun in a full circle, taking in each dusty corner. "After it's has a thorough cleaning, that is."

Her housekeeper nodded furiously. "I'll get to work on it right away, *señora*."

Meg frowned. "Is there no one who can help you?"

"Of course. I can get a few of the grooms to help me." The housekeeper darted a harried glance around them. "My own son included."

"Very well. Please see to it my painting and sculpting supplies are moved up here once it is clean. Oh! And my sewing machine." She couldn't wait to get back to tinkering with it.

Valentina nodded and bobbed a curtsey.

Satisfied by how suitable the space was for her needs, Meg made her way back downstairs to discover her new husband was missing.

A man named Miguel tried to explain in broken English how he had been called back to work.

Meg nodded regally at him. "And who might you be, sir?"

"My husband." Valentina took a protective step in front of him. "I fear he does not speak good English, *señora*, but I am happy to interpret."

Delighted to make the acquaintance of the man who would be commencing construction on her new dressing room, Meg eagerly led them to the master bedchamber to describe the project she envisioned. By extending the room, they could add both a sitting area and a dressing room. With much gesturing for Miguel's sake, she mimed where she wanted bars and hooks for hanging items, shelves for stacking hats and shoes, and drawers for stowing scarves, jewelry, and other accessories.

The man nodded often, scratched his head a few times, and muttered something to his wife in Spanish. They chattered back and forth in a manner that made their mistress suspect they were not in full agreement on the topic.

Valentina caught her eye at one point. "My husband would be most delighted to build your dressing room!" she assured with a sharp nod at him. Two bright spots of pink rode high on her coppery cheeks.

"How much will it cost?" Meg demanded.

The couple shared another heated exchange. "No extra money," Valentina declared with a steely light in her black eyes. "My husband says *Señor* Shad pays him more than enough. He believes there is plenty of lumber and stucco in the storage sheds, which means he can get started right away."

"*Gracias.*" Meg clasped her hands in exultation, beaming her gratitude at the couple. "Now, if you will excuse me." She made her way to the kitchen next. The dinner hour was fast approaching. It was past time for their tête-à-tête.

A very round, pale woman was silently peeling potatoes in a shadowy corner of the room. She was nearly as wide as she was tall. Her thin, white hair was scraped into a knobby bun atop her head, making it look rather like the lid of a cookie jar.

She spared Meg only the briefest of glances. "You must be

lost, miss," she stated brusquely and continued peeling. "The dining room is next door. I'll forgive you the mistake this once, but don't be making it again, you hear?"

A huff of disbelief flew from Meg's lips. So this was Tandy Holmes whom Valentina was so fearful of disturbing. "This farmhouse is entirely too small for anyone to become lost inside it," she retorted with enough starch in her voice to make a dozen aprons stand upright on their own.

Tandy's gaze flickered back to hers, and she sucked in a sharp breath as if barely holding on to her temper.

This would never do. Meg mustered up her sunniest smile and prepared to give the woman every opportunity to redeem herself before going to battle with her. "I am here to assist with dinner. If you'll take a moment to show me around, I'd be much obliged."

The woman threw her knife down and shot to her feet. "I do not know who you think you are, miss—"

She cut the ill-mannered woman short with a flick of a hand. "I'm Mr. Nicholson's new wife. However, something tells me you already know that." She spared the cook a shrewd once-over, not caring the least for the thunder gathering in her pale features or the defiance in her stance.

"Well, I never!" If such a thing were possible, Meg was certain steam would be billowing from the woman's ears.

"My home. My kitchen," she continued. "Either you can do as I have so kindly requested, or there is the way out, madame." She pointed at the door leading from the kitchen to the small washroom. Beyond it was the outdoors. Never before had she felt so much like her father's daughter. Part of her was mortified at the thought; the other part of her knew it was necessary to establish her authority. Otherwise, she would never be taken seriously by Shad's household staff, especially by the difficult ones like Tandy.

For an answer, the cook snatched off her apron, threw it on the floor, and stomped from the room.

With a sigh of resignation, Meg picked up the woman's apron and draped it over the high-back chair she'd vacated. So much for a tour of the kitchen and pantry. It looked as if dinner was entirely up to her now.

By the bottom of the hour, she'd cut her thumb — thrice, sent countless numbers of the slippery root vegetables skidding across the floor, and burnt the entire batch of potatoes atop the wood-burning stove. She retreated in distressed silence to her bedchamber, stomach growling with hunger pains. To her eternal gratitude, Shad did not return home that evening to witness her failed attempt at dinner.

Or the next night.

Or the next.

CHAPTER 5: LADY OF THE MANOR

*D*etermined not to admit culinary defeat, Meg rose early each morning and made her way to the kitchen. The first morning, the room reeked so strongly of burnt potatoes she had to place a clothespin over her nose in order to make it bearable. She dismally regarded the pan holding their charred remains resting in the middle of a long preparation counter.

Since the room was empty, she didn't bother suppressing a loud groan of frustration as she went to work. Alas, no matter how much she scraped and scrubbed, the pan remained black and caked with crusty potato corpses.

"Lord, give me strength." She paused to wipe a weary hand across her forehead, not realizing she left a sooty streak there. A glance down at her favorite green wool gown alerted her to the fact she'd somehow managed to smear soot from her bodice to her waist. "I will not give up. I will not give up," she chanted through clenched teeth.

A light clearing of a male throat had her spinning around.

Carlo, the young groom she'd met the day before, stood there with his felt cap rolled in his hands. "*Hola,*

Señora Meg. My mum mentioned you might could use some assistance this morning." He was a lad of fifteen or sixteen years with a star-struck cast to his dark, expressive eyes.

Mercy! She could understand how he might have been impressed with her east coast finery yesterday, but today? She glanced down at her soiled gown, finding nothing whatsoever for him to admire. Rolling her eyes, she waved at the scorched pan of potatoes she was beginning to view as her mortal enemy. "I burnt the potatoes; and for the life of me, I cannot get the dratted pan cleaned up." It was as if the charred potatoes had some maniacal, demonic hold on the pitiful pan.

Carlo grinned. "Have you tried soaking it in vinegar, *señora?*"

"Vinegar!" She moved across the room to rummage in the pantry. "At this juncture, I am willing to try anything, my friend."

His grin widened, and he sauntered across the room to deftly remove a blue glass jar from a silver bucket. "This is what you are looking for, *señora*."

She reached for the blue bottle, uncapped it, removed the clothes pin from her nose, and gave a tentative sniff. The vinegar fumes were so strong they wrinkled her entire face and made her eyes water. "Whew!" She held the bottle away from her. "I believe you're right." It smelled like it could peel rock off the side of a mountain. She started to tip the bottle over the crusted-over pan, but Carlo shook his head vehemently.

"*No, señora*. Outside." He reached for the pan.

She willingly handed it over and held open the door for him while he carried it outdoors. She watched as he dosed the pan with vinegar, and the pesky little burnt potatoes began to sizzle and slowly peel away from the metal. When she leaned over the pan with her scrub brush, he shook his head again.

"Let it set, *señora*. It is time to peel more potatoes and feed the staff."

Her eyes slowly widened in horror. "Please, please, please assure me I am the only person who went to bed hungry last night." She'd no idea the crabby cook she'd sent on her way had been preparing a meal for the entire staff!

He slowly shook his head. "Fear not, *Señora* Meg. It was well worth missing a meal to see the horrible Tandy go."

"Oh, dear heavens!" A bout of lightheadedness seized her. When she swayed on her feet, Carlo steadied her shoulders and led her back inside to the high-back chair in the corner of the room. "Sit, *señora*."

He stirred the coals in the hearth, blew on them until flames flickered to life, and added a few sticks of wood to coax them to a full roar. Next, he set a teapot swinging over the fire. In minutes, the room was filled with the enticing scents of cinnamon and chocolate. He poured her a cup and served her with a princely flourish and a twinkle.

She sipped on the thick, chocolaty beverage. "It is divine," she sighed. "What is it called?"

"Champurrado, *señora*. It is a drink from the old country. My father made it and his father before him."

"Mexico?" she asked softly.

"*Si, señora.*"

He bustled around the room while she drank, clearing the countertop of the mess she'd left the evening before. When he returned, he was bearing a heaping bowl of potatoes and two knives.

"Watch." He set the bowl of potatoes on a low table between them and settled on a stool across from her. "This is how you peel vegetables without drawing blood."

She set down her mug and held up her two bandaged

hands with a rueful chuckle. "You mean this wasn't supposed to happen?"

He shook his head, dark eyes gleaming merrily, and began to peel.

She leaned closer, frowning in concentration as she studied his movements. Then she picked up her knife and tried again. To her intense irritation, the more of the potato she peeled, the slicker it became. And just like before, the vegetable shot out from her fingers.

Carlo neatly caught it before it hit the ground, finished peeling it, and dropped it back in the bowl.

"What am I doing wrong?" she cried.

"Try again, *señora*." Carlo handed her another potato.

At the pace she worked, he easily peeled five to six potatoes for every one of hers. Shaking her head, she dogged onward for what felt like hours until the entire bowl was peeled.

She followed him back outdoors and watched while he pumped water from the well. "Let me," she said and motioned for him to show her how. It took a few tries, but he soon had her pumping water into the bucket.

"I did it!" she crowed with a bounce of sheer joy.

He shook his head at her, looking like he was trying not to laugh, and proceeded to rinse the potatoes with the water she'd pumped.

"What comes next? she demanded eagerly as they returned to the kitchen.

"Shredding, *señora*." He produced a grate and demonstrated how to rub the raw potatoes up and down it in order to shred them into tiny hair-like pieces.

She was amazed at how quickly the pile of potato shreds grew. The only trick was keeping her fingertips out of the way as the potato in her hand grew smaller, so she did not shred them as well. "What on earth are we going to do with this?" She gestured at the enormous, fluffy pile of potato shreds.

"Fry up a mess of potato cakes," he announced. "They're a staff favorite, *señora*."

She shadowed him while he unearthed a large iron skillet and slapped a dollop of bacon grease into it. In seconds, he had the grease popping enticingly over the stove. He threw fistfuls of potato shreds into the grease, patting them flat with a long wooden spoon.

Meg's stomach rumbled as the scents of bacon and browning potatoes filled the room.

It took a full half hour or more to prepare two heaping platters. When the last of the shreds had been transformed into Carlo's marvelous cakes, he motioned for her to pick up one of the platters. He picked up the other, and together they sailed into the dining room to serve the breakfast feast.

To Meg's surprise, the long dining room table was lined with ranch workers. She'd not heard any commotion as they'd entered the room and settled themselves, five on one bench and four on the other. Valentina was the only other woman present.

"Let us pray." Meg set her platter in the center of the table, stepped back, and bowed her head. The ranch workers immediately grew silent and bowed their heads as well.

"Heavenly Father." She could not recall ever being so thankful for a meal in her entire sojourn on this earth. Her voice trembled slightly as she blessed their breakfast. "In your most Holy Name. Amen."

In unison, the ranch workers made the sign of the cross against their chests and raised their heads.

She was so pleased with her first successfully prepared meal that she remained standing, wanting nothing more than to watch the staff devour it. Alas, none of them started eating. Instead, they watched her expectantly.

Ah. She perceived they were waiting for their mistress to be seated. She swiftly took her place at the foot of the table. "Please." She gestured at the food. "Eat."

Miguel, whose dark gaze had been darting between her and his son with no small amount of disapproval, dug into his plate of cakes with gusto.

Carlo left the room and returned with two steaming teapots. The delicious champurrado was passed around and poured. At one point during the meal, he leaned closer to Meg. "Tomorrow we will bake bread, *señora.*"

True to his word, he gave her a lesson on baking the next morning, in which he produced tray after tray of perfect golden loaves with swirls of steam rising from their centers. Her first attempt resulted in a flat lump that resembled the clay-packed trails traversing the ranch.

Her patient mentor did not look the least bit discouraged. "Try again, *señora.*" They fell into a pattern of him cooking the bulk of their meals while she performed one disastrous culinary experiment after another.

During each meal, his father glared at them from across his plate. Meg had no idea what she had done to earn his ire, though it was clear he was displeased with her. She tried not to let it bother her as she doggedly continued to learn her way around the kitchen.

As the weekend approached, she began to fret about facing her husband again. Valentina and Carlo assured her it was typical of him to be gone all week and that she could expect him to be home on the weekends. They claimed his job as a telegraph clerk required long hours. Still, being married to a man who was absent so often — and on his wedding night, no less — felt a little disconcerting. His unconventional work schedule was certainly going to take some getting used to.

A glance down at her gown had her yelping in surprise,

making the ranch hands seated on either side of her jolt in alarm. "I'm an absolute fright," she muttered and fled the room. It was Friday, and her husband could arrive home by the afternoon. She didn't want him seeing her in the umpteenth gown she'd ruined this week.

Valentina followed her as she'd fallen into the habit of doing, clucking in alarm. "Wait, *señora*. I will assist you with your dress, your bath, whatever you wish."

The urgent tenor of her voice gave Meg pause. She halted in mid stride and slowly turned to face her housekeeper. "I did not ask for your assistance this time," she noted coolly. She'd been working hard all week to break old habits and develop new ones — the habits of normal, average, non-wealthy people — which included *not* relying on a lady's maid for every tie and button.

"*Si*, but I am happy to help. Always." The woman wrung her hands in agitation.

"Perhaps." Meg held up one finger. "But it is more than that, isn't it? You seem to be following me," she accused.

Valentina gasped and paled. "But I must, *señora*! It is my duty."

"Pshaw." *That was a bunch of stuff and nonsense if she'd ever heard any!* She rolled her eyes and tried to wave her away, but her housekeeper bustled around her to open her bedchamber door.

A blast of cold air greeted them.

Meg gaped at the missing wall of her bedchamber. Miguel and his companions had wasted no time in commencing on the addition she'd requested. The frame for the new walls was already raised, awaiting the plank siding and stucco to seal it in.

"I'll pour up a bath and lay out a fresh change of clothes." Valentina scurried into the room to scoop up soaps, lotions, and a towel. "Then I'll assist you with your hair."

Suspicion rolled through Meg's chest. "He's making you spy on me, isn't he? My husband. He ordered you to watch my every move, didn't he?" Come to think of it, she couldn't recall very many spaces of time Valentina had been out of sight since her arrival.

The woman shook her head in distress. "It is not like that, *señora*. He is very afraid for your safety is all. He asked me, well, all of us to be vigilant until he can return with proper protection for you."

"Bodyguards?" *So that is what my new husband is up to?* Fully incensed at his highhandedness, Meg firmly shut her bedchamber door and faced her housekeeper. "I will not be held prisoner in my own home." Despite her valiant effort to control her emotions, her voice cracked.

"There, there, *señora*."

But the damage was done. All week long, Meg had put every ounce of effort into proving herself to her husband, and all the while he'd been working behind her back to hire bodyguards she didn't need or want. He hadn't even given her a chance before tossing her aside like a helpless ninny. She backed towards the four-poster bed until her calves bumped the railing. She blindly took a seat and wept for the duplicitous nature of the man she'd married. She wept for the many cuts on her hands, for all the dresses she'd ruined, for the loneliness she could not seem to outrun, and for the family she was apparently never going to have — not even with her new husband. It was a hard blow to absorb.

Valentina's feet were rooted to the floor in front of the dresser where she watched her mistress in stunned silence.

As abruptly as her tears had exploded, they just as quickly evaporated. Meg rose with a jerk of her skirts from the bed, no longer caring how badly soiled her gown was or how smudged her cheeks were. "I am heading to my studio. See that no one follows me. I wish to be alone."

She flounced from the room in high dudgeon. Shad could breeze back to his blasted ranch like a returning hero and eat cold chicken in the kitchen, for all she cared. She was finished trying to please a man who wasn't capable of seeing her as anything more than a burden to his perfectly organized existence.

The attic wasn't exactly a glorious exodus to new worlds and adventures, but it was empty of everyone save her. For now, it was the closest she could get to freedom.

She climbed the stairs, surprised to discover how toasty warm it was despite the lack of a wood stove or fireplace. Another surprise greeted her at the top of the stairs. Someone had meticulously cleaned the space. The air smelled of cleaning agents, and the window panes sparkled. Someone had also unpacked and set out her twin easels as well as her white column for sculpting. Her new sewing machine was neatly tucked in one corner on a low table. Her faded and scuffed carousel horse graced the opposite corner.

Her benevolent attendant had even gone so far as to set a blank canvas on the first easel. Her paints were neatly lined up on a nearby tray table. She stared for several gratified moments. For some reason, the kind and thoughtful display of her most adored possessions made her want to weep all over again.

It was through eyes glassy with unshed tears that she began to paint the sliver of landscape she glimpsed through the dormer window. She painted exactly what she saw, which meant each paint stroke took on a blurry, muted appearance. Instead of the window separating her from the distant canyons and mesas, she painted prison bars.

She lost all track of time while she worked. Minutes must have turned into hours, because the mid-afternoon sun faded to the deeper, darker glow of evening. She didn't stop until the last stroke of clouds was dabbed on her canvas. When she stood back and surveyed her work, she was forced to admit it was quite possibly the finest piece she'd ever produced.

Born of despair and hopelessness, the scene had a watery cast to it. Such was her view of the world beyond the windowpanes when her eyes were swimming with tears. The prison bars were symbolic, but they felt as real as if the cold metal was pressed against her hands and cheeks.

"Meg!" Shad's voice resonated across the attic space, shaking her to her core.

Her husband was home.

She froze with her back to him, unable to face him or anyone else in her shattered state.

"I hope you will forgive me for leaving you alone the first few nights of our marriage." He cleared his throat. "I couldn't breathe easy until I could provide you with proper protection."

Meaning he'd returned with the bodyguards Valentina had warned her about. She was his prisoner now just as she'd been her father's prisoner all those years.

His boots stepped closer. "I don't suppose you have an explanation for the missing wall in our bedchamber?"

"I needed a dressing room," she responded dully. It no longer mattered. Nothing mattered anymore.

"And I suddenly find myself missing a cook."

"She was a despicable creature." Meg spat out the words. "Everyone was glad to see her go."

"So it seems." He sounded self-recriminating. "It appears she was taking advantage of my long absences."

Her heart sank to a new low at the reminder she'd married a man who did not intend to spend much time at home with her.

"I am sorry for the cuts on your hands and your ruined gowns." This time his voice sounded much closer, as if he was standing directly behind her.

Meg lifted her chin in defiance. Her back remained turned to him, which meant the only way he could have known those things was if Valentina had confided in him. The woman could paint her inexcusable behavior in any color she wanted, but spying was still spying.

"I did not mean to incur your wrath by asking my staff to look after you in my absence. My only thought was to protect you, Meg." His hands settled on her slender waistline.

She trembled but held her ground. "If I'd known you intended to make me a prisoner in your home, I would have never left Boston," she snapped.

"I know." His voice was low and gentle, infused with a heart-wrenching dose of regret. She did not doubt he was ruing the day he'd written the letter to summon her west. "Alas, I cannot undo what is already done. We are married, Meg. Before God and man, you are mine to protect."

"More's the pity!" she said beneath her breath, hardly caring whether he heard her. "I am your prisoner now, just as I was my father's prisoner."

His ragged intake of breath assured her he'd heard. "It may seem like that, yes, but I will not step aside and leave you to the vultures!" he seethed. "You cannot ask that of me, Meg. You can't!" His hands moved up to her shoulders, spinning her around.

They stared in agony at each other.

She lowered her lashes. "Go ahead and gloat. Say I am not cut out for life in the savage west." She wasn't cut out for life anywhere outside her gilded cage, apparently. "Say you were right."

"I cannot." He cupped her face in one warm palm and tipped it up to his. "Because I was wrong. Very, very wrong."

She blinked and hated herself a little when the movement jarred loose a lone tear. She'd thought she'd already wept every last drop from her body. "You were not!" she hissed.

"Just look at me!" Her gown was stained. Her hair was in disarray. The cuts on her hands were still healing.

"I am!" he snarled. "I'm looking at a very stubborn, very determined woman. I'll admit I had my doubts when you stepped off the train, but no longer. You are stronger than I ever imagined, more resilient than any person I've ever met. The good Lord could not have sent a more perfect match for me."

"What?" she cried. Of all the things she speculated he might say, this was not among them. More tears streaked down her face. "You do not regret marrying me?" Had she truly misjudged his intentions so badly?

"Not for a second!"

She was too starved for validation to maintain her stoney resistance. The fervency in his voice and the admiring light in his eyes proved her undoing.

On a sob, she launched herself at him.

His arms encircled her like a safe and tender haven. He crushed his mouth to hers.

CHAPTER 6: GATHERING STORM

Meg's lips were swollen from crying and tasted of tears, but they also tasted of cautious hope and something more that incited every masculine instinct in him. It humbled and enthralled him that this lovely, accomplished, brilliant young woman was willing — however reluctantly — to entrust herself to his care.

Shad could only hope and pray he was up to the task of shielding and protecting her from any danger that might already be headed their way. He didn't agree with her for one second that severing her ties to Gladstone Trans-Atlantic Shipping was enough to remove the ongoing threat to her personal safety. She was as wealthy as royalty. That fact alone would continue to make her a target.

He plunged a hand into her mussed curls, reveling in the silken drag of strands across his callused fingers. All money matters aside, she was a treasure in her own right; she was brave and beautiful, innocent and good. It was up to him now to keep her so.

In many ways, he was in awe of her. In the short time she'd inhabited his home, she'd won over the heart of an unapproachable stray animal, rid his household staff of one very bad apple, and had the ranchers leaping to move entire walls for her. As for him, he was ready to throw himself bodily between her and any number of dangers.

His new wife was quite simply proving herself to all of them to be worth it.

He raised his head to gaze into her tear-swollen eyes. "I will find a way to set you free," he promised. "I swear it."

He could tell by the soft and wondrous light that crept into her bruised hazel eyes that she wanted to believe him. "You may give away every penny of my wealth with my blessing." Her voice shook. "Or burn it!"

He nodded and touched his forehead to hers, cradling her face in his hands. "I have some ideas, but I must beg your patience. What you ask of me will take a little time."

"I have nothing but time," she assured him sadly.

"Not true." He raised his head and brushed away the dampness beneath her eyes with the pads of his thumbs. "You have me."

She gave him the faintest of smiles. "Thank you, Shad."

He smiled tenderly at her. "If I could freeze this moment in time, I would. I would stay up here with you…like this… forever." He bent to brush his lips against hers once more. "But I cannot."

The tiny smile she'd given him disappeared. "Your job as a telegraph operator calls, eh?" Her lashes fluttered down, making it impossible to see what she was thinking. However, her tone was dry.

"I wish things were that simple." He continued to cradle her face in his hands until her lashes rose once more. Though it went against everything he'd been taught in his career as an undercover marshal, he knew it was time to give her a reason to believe in him. "I hired a new employee earlier this week, Bram Fairfield. He's the son of a miner out at that yellow diamond mine in Hope's Landing. A very promising up and comer. A quick learner. It won't be long before he can take over the running of the daily operations at the office."

Her expression brightened, making him loathe to continue what he had to say.

"I had to hire help, because my current assignment is requiring longer and longer hours in the field."

Her lovely, pencil-perfect blonde brows came together. "I'm afraid I do not understand."

He wanted to bare his soul to her, share every secret. Alas, he was already admitting more than he should. "I was sent to Headstone in the hopes of intercepting various communications flying across the west as part of an undercover investigation."

Her brilliant mind did not require him to spell out every word. Her brows smoothed as understanding flooded her expression. "And you succeeded."

"I did."

"You're not really a telegraph operator," she accused, pushing away from him to fist her slender hands on her hips.

It felt insanely good to be sharing some his deepest, darkest confidences with someone else at long last. "Well, now," he teased, cocking a brow at her and mimicking her saucy stance with his hands on his own hips. "A good many citizens in Headstone might disagree with you. I believe I've done a standup job of running their telegraph office."

"You know what I mean," she retorted tartly, reaching over to stab a finger against his chest. "If I had to venture a guess, I'd say you're federal law enforcement."

He caught her hand and held it to his heart, grinning. "As it turns out, transmitting telegrams is a rather clever way to stay informed. It is precisely how I learned about the existence of the Boomtown Mail Order Brides Company."

She flushed a lovely shade of pink that made him want to kiss her again. "I see," she said in a breathy voice.

"Transmitting telegrams also helped me pinpoint exactly where a human trafficking ring is holding a pocket of missing Mexican immigrants. We suspect there are other victims — many, in fact — but this was the first big breakthrough in our case." May the Lord be praised, it had been a long time coming. More than three years, to be exact. Long enough for his superiors to start making sounds about giving up on his current location and sending him elsewhere. It had taken much convincing on his part to make them stay the course. "I've been tasked to help raid their facility tomorrow." Technically, he and his team were scheduled to commence their raid in the middle of the night. According to their reconnaissance work, this was when they could expect the next guard change at the mine, leaving their entrances and exits the most vulnerable.

Meg stepped closer. "It sounds dangerous." Her frown was back. "Do you really have to go? We just got married, Shad. Don't we deserve a few days together, at least, before..." Her voice dwindled beneath his touch.

He traced her chin with a finger, willing her to understand, needing her to understand. "It's the job I chose, Meg. I had no family, no connections at the time I pinned on my badge. Growing up, I'd always dreamed of doing something meaningful with my life, something that mattered." He'd longed to erase how discarded and unworthy he'd felt as an orphan. As it turned out, there weren't many folks in the country wanting to adopt teens.

Her eyes turned a luminous shade of blue and green. "You matter to me, Shad. Very much."

Her words took his breath away. This was exactly what he'd hoped for when he penned his letter to Jordan Branson. Meg was everything he'd dreamed of and more — a miracle from above — but marrying her was forcing him to a crossroads he'd not foreseen. She wasn't some delightful little secret he could keep tucked away on his ranch as he originally and foolishly hoped. She was his partner, his perfect mate, a woman who needed and deserved to be protected as much as the poverty-stricken immigrants being pressed into service at the Traxton Silver Mine on the outskirts of town. At some point soon, he was going to have to make a decision between her and his job. Only one of them could come first. He realized that now.

"You matter to me, too, Meg. I want this. I truly do. I want us." He wanted a family so badly his chest ached from the intensity of it. He wanted it right now, today, before the investigation ended. He wanted a real wedding night with her and everything that came with it. He wanted to come home to her every evening after work. He wanted it all — companionship, love, trust, intimacy, children — more than one…with her.

"Then choose us," she begged softly. "Choose me."

"I will." He closed his eyes, praying for the wisdom and courage to see his current mission through to the end. "I will return to you when this job is over, and things will be different. I promise."

"I believe you." Her arms slid around his middle, and she pressed her cheek to his leather vest. "In the meantime, I ask that you do what you must without taking unnecessary risks. You're no longer without family or connections, Shadrack Nicholson." She slid her left hand up his chest, moving her fingers this way and that. The opal and diamonds on her ring finger caught the evening light, making the opal glow and the diamonds flicker like tiny flames.

"I have to go now." He hated the necessity of leaving her another night, but it couldn't be helped. His posse of marshals needed to raid the silver mine before the owners had the opportunity to move their fugitives again. He'd long suspected the mine was merely a front for trafficking. They hadn't produced enough silver in the past year to keep a kitten fed. With their proximity to the Southwestern Railroad spur, he suspected they were moving their prisoners across country in cargo containers.

"Very well." Meg's voice was soft and trusting. There were no more tears, no protests, no frivolous cajoling to detain him from the inevitable. He adored her for her show of inner strength, for not making his job any harder than it already was.

Which made it all the more difficult to leave her.

She tipped her face up to his. "I confess I'm not practiced in saying goodbye to my new husband. You'll have to show me how it is done."

He found it difficult to think with her soft, lush mouth so close to his. Maybe she wasn't above employing a few female wiles to detain him, after all. The notion flattered him to no end.

"I don't want to leave you, Meg. I don't want to say goodbye." He didn't dare risk another kiss, or he might not make it back in time to his rally point with the other marshals.

"Then do not say anything else at all." She raised her head from his chest and gave him a gentle shove. "Just go. Quickly." She made a shooing motion with her hands. "So you can hurry back to me."

The light and promise in her eyes made his heart thud like a drum on a parade field.

He slowly backed away from her, each step he placed between them causing him real, tangible pain. It took a superhuman effort to drag his gaze from hers and make his exit down the stairs.

His heart sang as he left the house in search of Miguel. For the first time in his career, he would have a wife waiting for him when he returned — an exorbitantly lovely, intelligent, and adoring one. The thought gave him so much joy it was a wonder his heart didn't burst.

Miguel was waiting for him in the main barn with his favorite Missouri Foxtrotter already saddled and geared up.

Thanks to years of training, he was fluent in Mexican Spanish, so Miguel didn't have to flounder through his repertoire of broken English to converse with him.

"I don't know how long I'll be gone this time."

Miguel nodded and tightened the strap on one of his packs. "God be with you, *amigo*. Your hired guns and I will look after the *señora.*"

They weren't just any hired guns. Shad had enlisted the help of some of the toughest renegades in the west. Their unorthodox alliance one of the benefits of being an undercover federal marshal. All three were ex-*Rurales* of the rural mounted Mexican police force living on the down-low in the surrounding canyons, and all three owed him their lives.

Confident they would grant him this one favor to keep the occupants of his ranch safe in his absence, Shad leaped astride his stallion and held his closest friend's gaze steadily. "She is my life, Mig. She is my Valentina and my Carlo."

Miguel reached up to clasp him hand to forearm in the salutation of a fellow soldier.

They nodded grimly at each other, and Shad dug in his heels. Diablo tossed his shiny black mane and took off across the sandy grasslands with a harsh whinny. It wasn't his first mounted raid, and he seemed to understand they were riding into battle. He easily scaled the pasture fences, making it unnecessary to take a detour around the farm.

Shad bent low over his powerfully corded neck, giving the glorious creature full rein. With Diablo's unique four-step gait, they made excellent time. The dusty canyons and red mesas seemed to fly past. At his best estimate, they were traveling nigh on ten miles per hour, which would put him at their rally point before sundown.

Please, God. The twenty-mile ride gave him plenty of time to think and pray. *I give my wife, my ranch help, my livestock, and my home into your hands. Protect them while I am away. All our hope is in you.*

Guilt flooded him with each mile that separated him and Meg. For the first time in his adult years, he found himself second-guessing himself. Had he done the right thing by leaving his new bride in the care of Miguel and the hired expatriots? Wasn't it his duty to protect her himself? Hadn't he vowed to do exactly that during their wedding ceremony?

He tried to console himself with the fact that there were no known and immediate threats to his wife's safety — at least no more than the ones she'd lived with her entire twenty-one years. *Good heavens!* For a rich girl, her life hadn't been easy.

He couldn't imagine what it must have been like for her to be raised by a constantly changing guard of perfect strangers. From his recent exchange of telegrams with her family attorney, he'd learned she'd not been free to attend school like a normal child, to have friends, to play tag or hide-and-go-seek. She'd been kept in the velvet chains of wealth behind high stone walls with thick iron doors by a father who was rarely home.

Herman Gladstone had been a powerful shipping baron, well feared by the pirate fleets roaming the Atlantic, and revered like something of a god by the law-abiding subsidiaries who ran his cargo. His only Achilles heel had been his daughter; and during his lifetime, none of his enemies had been able to reach her. But, oh, at what a cost!

The man had kept the one person in the world he loved imprisoned like a lightning bug in a jar. Shad didn't want to make the same mistake. There had to be a better way to protect Meg, a way that didn't stifle her artistic temperament and strip her of every last vestige of personal freedom.

The kisses they'd shared still burned on his lips, and the hopeful pleading in her eyes still tugged at his heart. He'd meant what he said about finding a way to set her free. *Show me the way, Lord. Give me the right opportunities and the wisdom to help the woman you've entrusted to my care.*

The rally point shivered on the horizon and took shape in the form of an outcropping of sandstone. The way the wind and sand had chiseled away at it over the years made it resemble the hollowed-out entrance to a cave. However, it was merely an outcropping that led to nowhere. Tonight it would shelter the marshals' horses while they crept their way inside the silver mine located a quarter mile farther down the ridge line. They'd managed to get their hands on a six-month-old sketch of the mine, so they had an idea where the trafficking records were most likely being stored. They'd also narrowed down the location of the prisoners to the two tunnels closest to the train depot.

Shad slowed his horse as he spied the silhouette of a man pacing beneath the sandstone shelter. Fairly certain he was visible within the glow of sunset, he brought Diablo to a halt and waited for the signal to approach. U.S. Marshal Jason Peck from Paradise Valley was serving as their look-out this evening. Their agreed upon signal was three flashes from a lantern being covered and uncovered in quick succession.

When the signal wasn't given, he slowly backed his horse away, scanning the surrounding landscape for any sign of trouble. The desert evening was ominously quiet — too quiet. The surrounding ridges were choked with paloverde and mesquite. There should have been the raucous call of a woodpecker at least, not such dead and heavy silence.

Shad lightly yanked on his reins to send Diablo cantering over the low rise leading to the nearest mesa. Though it would expose his position a little more than he preferred, it would be an excellent vantage point from which to survey what was happening below him.

He didn't make it to the flat top of the mesa before the first shot sounded.

CHAPTER 7: CHANGE OF PLANS

The bullet fell short of him by a good twenty yards or more, kicking up sand where it landed. Concerned about the plight of Jason Peck and the two other marshals he was supposed to meet up with, Shad turned his horse to face the direction of the shot. Reaching behind him to unbuckle his pack, he pulled out his Porro prism binoculars and held them up with one hand to take a closer look.

Alarm pooled in his gut at the sight of two bodies crumpled like rag dolls in the sand. He couldn't tell if the men were injured or dead, but one thing was clear. Somehow the rogue mine operators had gotten the jump on them. Their rally point was compromised.

He was far enough away from the ambush to have a healthy head start if he chose to retreat, but the thought of scrapping the mission made him taste bile. They'd invested too much in this investigation and come too close to victory to give up now. Giving up would also mean the casualties lying out there in the sand had been neutralized in vain. The only way to give their sacrifice meaning was to complete the mission.

If their enemies were familiar with marshal code, they were probably expecting the survivors to scrap their mission at this point. The problem with retreating and regrouping, however, was that the prisoners in the mine would be long gone by the time they returned. Worse yet, Shad might be followed, potentially leading a dangerous set of criminals straight to his own doorstep.

And to Meg.

The best course of action was to adapt and carry on. He couldn't prove it yet, but he had a strong hunch where the rogue miners were taking their prisoners next. Since there were no bodies of water nearby, it only made sense they were transporting them by rail.

Keeping his horse in the shadows of the ridge, he circled the mesa and arrived at the first mine entrance he and his team had originally planned to investigate. Sure enough, a line of humans were being marched in single file in the direction of the railroad tracks.

Another peek through his binoculars verified their jerky, shallow steps were due to the fact their ankles were bound with a short stretch of rope, making it impossible for them to run.

Or escape...

Movement against the canyon wall to his left gave Shad pause. Someone else was out there. He trained his lenses in that direction and was greatly relieved to glimpse the squared-off features of Jason Peck. He raised his thumb to indicate he was uninjured and was overjoyed to see Jason raise his thumb in response.

Holding his right hand at times in a straight line and other times in a fist, he signed his next move to Peck in Morse code. They were too outnumbered to ambush the ambushers. The only way to save the Mexican fugitives at this juncture was to make their move farther from the station, which meant they would need to board a moving train.

Jason signed back a negative response. He thought it was too risky, but Shad reiterated his plan. Not only was it their best option, it was their last viable one before the window of opportunity closed forever on rescuing this particular group of prisoners.

A whistle blew in the distance, indicating the cargo train in question was making its way to the station. The line of prisoners was halted. Since the depot was two to three blocks away, Shad could only assume the approaching train was sizable in length. He also guessed the cargo car they would be loaded on was nearer the back of the train than the front.

He was correct. The train blasted its way into the station with several bursts from its horns and a mighty squeal of brakes against the tracks. When fully stopped, it was long enough to stretch all the way to the line of prisoners. Shad watched and waited in the shadows until each of them was sealed inside the cargo car. He counted twelve in all. The door was shut and bolted behind them, indicating they were unaccompanied by guards. That was a good thing for what Shad and Peck had planned.

Then the long wait began. It was a particularly cold desert night, which made him grateful for the extra layers he'd worn. While he waited, he moved the pack containing the supplies he would need from his horse to his shoulders. Three o'clock faded to four, and four o'clock faded to five. It wasn't until nearly six in the morning that the train rumbled to life once more and began to edge its way out of the station.

Shad nudged Diablo into motion and followed the train for a good half mile while it ever so slowly picked up speed.

He waited until he was certain he was out of the rogue miners' sight before he made his move.

He left the shadows of the canyon wall and drew his horse alongside the accelerating train. He had to push Diablo hard to match its speed. He slowly rose to a crouching position atop his saddle, grateful to own such a well-trained mount. They'd practiced this exact maneuver dozens of times back on the ranch.

At just the right moment, he leaped onto the stairway of the caboose. For a split second, one foot remained airborne, but he quickly found purchase. He shouted to Diablo to keep running, repeating the command several times to ensure the creature understood.

Then he clambered to the roof of the car, ran the flat length of it, gauged the distance to the next roof, and jumped. This time he made a bruising landing on all fours and slid a few inches. He had to flex his wrists several times to make the tingling sensation go away. Then he jogged to the opposite end of the roof where his real work could finally begin.

The train was picking up speed and outpacing Diablo who continued to run. Shad knew he had to work quickly before the precious window of opportunity closed. His hands flew as he unwound the fuse of his black powder bomb and lowered it by a thin metal wire to the axle below. If his plan was to work, he needed to sever the last two cars from the rest of the train.

The hardest part of the task was keeping a match lit long enough in the draft wind to ignite the fuse. Perhaps it was only due to the fact he had Divine Providence on his side, but he managed to do so on the third try. The fire quickly traveled along the fuse. He barely had the time to scoot to the far end of the roof before the bomb exploded.

It took several more seconds to determine whether his

plan had worked. Only when Diablo started to catch up with the train car was he certain.

Thank you, Lord! He pushed up on his hands and knees and watched the rest of the train pull away, leaving behind the last two cars. It didn't take much longer after that for the unmanned cars to creak to a halt.

He half-shimmied, half-leaped from the roof of the car to the ground to examine the locking system on the cargo door. It was still too dim to see clearly. In the end, he opted to shoot off the lock. He threw open the door, and twelve pairs of eyes stared back at him, containing various degrees of fear and suspicion.

Speaking in Spanish, he motioned them forward. "Get out, *amigos*. You are free."

The first man to push out of the car was middle aged and emaciated. His expression was pinched, his skin papery thin, and his belly swollen. Shad pulled a canteen of water from his pack and handed it to him. "Drink, *amigo*."

Within minutes, Jason Peck caught up to him. "You're as loco as they come Nicholson," he chided, but there was no venom in his voice. His sharp blue gaze softened as it roved over the group of newly freed prisoners.

In all, there were seven men, three women, and two young boys no more than seven or eight years. Shad was incensed all over again at the terrors the small lads must have endured during their captivity. He recognized all too well their blank, glazed-over looks; it reminded him of his stint in the orphanage where he'd spent most of his days feeling hopeless and abandoned.

Peck hurried forward to help him cut the ropes binding their ankles and wrists. Two of the men immediately fled in the direction of the surrounding canyons.

"I said you were free," Shad assured the ten who

remained. "You are welcome to follow your comrades and run, or you can remain with U.S. Marshal Peck and myself."

Another man took off at a sprint, his bare feet kicking up sand with each stride.

"We can get you food, water, and shelter," Shad declared softly. "I own a ranch not far from here. You're welcome to board there as long as you wish. There are cabins, beds, even jobs for those who want them. Plus I can get you medical care." He eyed the emaciated man with concern. "And help you contact your loved ones. My resources are extensive." Virtually bottomless. He had the town's telegraph office at his disposal, an inside seat to local law enforcement, and access to funds his wife insisted he couldn't get rid of fast enough.

He and Peck handed out the rest of the provisions they had in their packs. In the end, eight of the Mexican immigrants they'd rescued from the train opted to join them on the long trek back to Headstone — three of the men, all three women, and both boys.

Shad placed the elderly man and one of the women on his horse. Peck lifted another one of the women to his mount and hefted the two small boys up in front of her. Gratitude brimmed in the eyes of their ragtag group of survivors as Shad and Peck marched alongside them on foot. They tasked two of the Mexican men to lead the horses so they could keep guard with their pistols at the ready, walking backwards a good amount of the time.

"Do you think any of them will be willing to testify against Traxton?" Peck asked him in undertones.

"Yes. I'm counting on it." With food, rest, and proper medical care, Shad expected there would be several in their party motivated to give their former captors' firm a mortal blow. He couldn't wait to use their testimonies against the Traxton brothers and the desperadoes aiding in their crimes.

The ensuing indictments were going to put a real crimp in their current machinations and hopefully put them behind bars for many years to come.

WHEN SHAD WAS NOT BACK HOME on Saturday morning, Meg's throat constricted with alarm. *He promised!* She sat up on the thick pile of blankets in the attic where she'd spent the night — against Valentina's many protests — and rubbed her eyes. *He promised to choose me. To choose us!*

And she'd believed him. Everything in his expression and stance had indicated his reluctance to leave her. *One last job,* he'd assured. *Then things will be different. I promise.* To her, that meant he'd return the soonest possible moment to begin the rest of their lives together.

His raid of the silver mine was supposed to be today, but something didn't feel right about that. If it wasn't until today, why couldn't he have spent the night at home in his own bed? Which most likely meant the raid had happened very early, or even last night.

Was the raid a success? Was he safe and well now? The possibility he might be lying on the ground somewhere in the lonesome desert, injured or worse, made it difficult for her to breathe. She wished with all her heart he'd taken with him the dangerous looking men he'd left to guard her. Something told her they'd be far more at ease in the saddle brandishing weapons than tromping around their home and outbuildings. Every time she caught sight of them, their expressions told her they were bored senseless.

As was she…

Fairly vibrating from the agitated energy coursing through her, she dressed in one of her favorite wool and silk winter gowns, a navy blue ensemble with gold piping around the neckline and sleeves and military-esque buttons running down the bodice. A ruffle of cream lace was tucked against her bosom for modesty's sake. Her hair dresser back in Boston had swept her blonde curls in all sorts of elaborate up-do's, but she didn't have the time or interest in bothering with such frivolity today. She tamed her curls as best she could and tied them back with a narrow blue ribbon.

Valentina met her at the bottom of the attic stairs. "Did you sleep well, *señora*? Were you warm enough?" She wrung her hands. "I cannot believe you insisted on sleeping on the floor up there. *Señor* Shad is going to wonder if my wits have gone a-wandering."

"I'm worried about him, Valentina!" She rounded on the woman, ignoring her fussing. "He should have been back by now."

"There, there, *señora*." Sympathy brimmed from her housekeeper's eyes. "You know his job requires long—"

"Meg!" She clasped the woman's shoulders, forcing them to look each other square in the face. "My name is Meg. I know I pranced in here a week ago acting all lady-of-the-manor, because that was all I knew how to be. But I am trying to change. Surely you see that."

She felt naked and exposed beneath the woman's cautious scan of her features.

When the woman didn't speak, she sighed. "What I'm trying to say is, I need a friend right now much more than I need a maid." Her arms slid back to her sides. "And you're the closest thing I have to one."

Valentina's simpering, subservient manner evaporated a few degrees. "Very well, Meg. I do not have many friends, either. There aren't many womenfolk around these parts, so I sure wouldn't mind it if we stuck together." The smile that lit her face transformed her from a staid, proper housekeeper to something far more lovely.

Meg blinked. Why, in a different gown, with her styled just so, and a touch of paint on her lips, Valentina would be a truly stunning creature! She tucked that thought away for future reference and drew in a deep breath. "Thank you, Valentina."

Pressing a hand to her chest, she confided, "I was raised to be a woman of faith, someone who prays; but this morning I couldn't pray. Nothing feels right at the moment. All I seem to be able to do is worry about my husband."

"It is because you care. I feel the same way about Miguel when he's out on those long cattle drives. I worry every second until he returns home safe." Valentina touched her arm. "Come. I have something to show you."

She led her through the kitchen where Carlo was kneading bread dough. He was up to his elbows in flour but looked sublimely happy in his work. The air was filled with the delectable scent of autumn stew rising from the hearth. Unless she was mistaken, she smelled venison, apples, and spice, which meant he was experimenting again. She adored his experiments; everyone at the ranch did. Nobody except his father seemed to object to his presence in the kitchen, and she intended to get to the bottom of that mystery soon.

"Good morning, Carlo." Meg forced a bit of false cheer to her voice. He didn't deserve to have his skin scalded off by her disgruntled state.

"*Hola, señora.*" He gave her a dusty salute and went back to kneading.

Valentina patted his arm as she passed but didn't stop to visit. "Come," she said again, beckoning to Meg.

Puzzled, she followed her housekeeper outside and down a hard-packed path leading to the scattering of cabins and cottages where the hired help lived. A brisk December breeze nipped at their clothing and hair, making her grateful when they stepped inside once again.

She gazed around the small cabin, drinking in the cozy atmosphere. It was the simplest abode she'd ever visited with plain, roughly hewn furniture bearing no adornments. The kitchen had a small stove on one side with a narrow butcher block counter next to it for food preparation. A square trestle table and three chairs were tucked against the opposite wall to complete the room. The tiny parlor adjoining the kitchen boasted a faded blue velvet couch with nearly threadbare cushions. Through a half-ajar door, she glimpsed a bed in the next room covered with a patchwork quilt.

"This is where I live, Meg." Valentina spread her hands. "It may not look like much to a woman of your means, but it's a castle compared to the hut where we lived in Mexico."

Meg sighed. "I lived in a mansion back in Boston, as big as a castle, but it never felt like half the home you've managed to create here." She moved to the fireplace to gaze at the painting mounted there. It was a fanciful, dissonant scene in bright passionate colors. The rider and his mustang were purposefully left in hazy silhouette form, so the viewer would focus on the energy and mood of the piece. "I like it," she mused softly. "It speaks to me."

"I've been wondering what you would think of it ever since I realized you were a painter yourself. Now I know."

"*You* painted this?" Meg spun around in delight to face her newfound friend.

"I did." She glanced away, flushing slightly. "I've never had any formal training, but…"

"You're a natural," Meg assured, returning her attention to the lively scene playing itself out on the canvas. "We should paint together sometime. Take our easels out on the open range and let our creativity soar."

"I would like that very much."

Meg closed her eyes. "But not today. I couldn't paint a single leaf if my life depended on it. Oh, Valentina!" She moved to the small picture window overlooking the front porch. "If Shad doesn't return soon, I'll shatter into a thousand pieces."

"He will come home." Her friend's tone was adamant. "He always does."

CHAPTER 8: CALL FOR HELP

Meg knew Valentina meant well, but she wasn't reassured. The morning turned overcast, and ugly clouds appeared. No rain fell, but thunder cracked and lightning flashed. The disturbance in the heavens stirred a vicious wind that whipped at the countryside, swirling sand and debris everywhere. It lasted a full hour before it died down.

As the grisly morning deepened to noon and noon faded to a much calmer evening, her agitation grew. "Something is wrong!" she insisted as the dinner hour approached. "I cannot continue to pretend otherwise." She paced the front porch with the impatience of a race horse pawing the ground before the gates opened.

"Patience," Valentina coaxed, coming to stand by her side. She slid her arm around Meg's waist. "Your husband has gone on many missions, and the good Lord has always seen to his safety."

Meg wanted to believe her, but she couldn't shake the feeling of unrest churning her insides. "It's so difficult to stand around, waiting and worrying." She wasn't accustomed to having anyone to worry about.

"Perhaps we should go inside to inspect the progress of the addition to your bedchamber?"

Meg knew her friend was only trying to distract her, but it wasn't working. She kept reminding herself she was a woman of vast financial resources. There had to be something she could do to help her husband, even if she was forced to do it from home. *Yes, indeed!* There was one thing in particular she could do to help him from a distance. She cast a sideways look at Valentina. "Speaking of my construction project, I presume that is how your husband is employing himself at the moment?"

Valentina straightened and dropped her arm. "But, of course. He's been working on the addition since dawn. Why do you ask?"

"I need to pay a visit to the telegraph office. I was hoping he would drive me there."

Her friend looked startled. "Your husband left strict orders for us to keep you safe here at the ranch. He's been nothing but generous and good to my family. Please do not ask Miguel to defy his wishes."

Meg swallowed a growl of frustration. "Then please ask him to drive into town and deliver a message for me." She clasped her hands beseechingly beneath her chin, feigning a lightness she did not feel. "I've an important matter in Boston I need to attend to. Since I'm stuck here at the ranch…" She wasn't above playing on the woman's sympathies for her plight to get what she wanted.

"Very well." Valentina nodded reluctantly. "If it will keep you here at the ranch, then I'll speak to my husband right away. Go ahead and prepare your message, my friend."

Meg dashed to her husband's desk in their bedchamber to scrawl a short telegram. She was surprised to note most of the planks were covering the new walls, and a trio of men were meticulously applying stucco. The addition was going up much quicker than she'd anticipated. The room smelled of sawdust, wet mud, paint, and progress.

Normally, she would have stopped to admire their work, but she was too busy addressing her note to Jordan Branson of the Boomtown Mail Order Brides Company. She hoped the Gallant Insurance Clause his agency advertised so proudly to their bridal candidates would apply to a missing groom as well. She quickly jotted her message, keeping it brief and to the point.

My husband is missing. STOP Please activate Gallant Insurance Clause. STOP Last known location: Traxton Silver Mine STOP Urgent!

Miguel met her in the hall outside her bedchamber. His coppery cheeks were chapped pink from the cold outdoors. Valentina was clinging to his brawny arm as if she'd dragged him all the way inside.

He eyed her with a mixture of curiosity and defiance. "You require my assistance, *señora?*"

"Just Meg, please. Call me Meg."

Some of the tightness left his expression.

"And, yes. Something urgent has come up. A family matter." She shoved her note in his calloused hands. "Please ride as fast as you can to the telegraph office, and tell Bram to send it right away." She swallowed hard. For all she knew, Shad's life might be depending on it.

He looked to his wife for help with her rapid tirade. She quickly interpreted. He nodded in understanding and lifted his gaze to Meg's once more.

She held his gaze steadily, though she felt like she was breaking on the inside. She couldn't explain it in rational terms, but she was convinced her husband needed help, today, right now.

"Please, Miguel." *Grant me this one favor, and I will never ask for another silly construction project so long as I live.*

Without speaking, he bent to deliver a hard kiss to his wife's mouth, doffed his hat at Meg, and took off at a jog.

"I thank you!" she called after him. *With all my heart.* Hot tears prickled behind her lids. Maybe she was being overly dramatic, but it felt good to be doing something at last instead of merely sitting around and waiting.

She and Valentina followed him to the porch. He disappeared inside the main barn and emerged at a full gallop on one of Shad's prized Missouri Fox Trotters. They watched until he rode from view.

"You are fortunate Miguel is so loyal to your husband." Her housekeeper's voice was dry, and the look she gave her was full of suspicion. "Perhaps, now that I've convinced him to do your bidding, you'll have the grace to share with your *friend* what you're really up to."

Meg raised and lowered her hands. "If you must know, I've ordered a rescue party."

"For whom?" Valentina asked carefully.

"For my husband, of course!" She shot her a gleeful smile. "I may be new to this town, but I am not without my resources."

"You cannot!" her friend gasped. "Or rather, you *should* not!"

"Too late. Even if I wanted to stop Miguel at this juncture — which I decidedly do not — no one could possibly catch up with him in time."

"B-but you're interfering with a federal investigation!"

"Aha!" Meg shook a finger at her, grin widening. "It appears I'm not the only one who's been keeping secrets. You know about him, do you not?" she declared slyly. "You know what he truly does for a living?"

Valentina's lips thinned. "Indeed, I do. We are the first family he rescued from the Traxtons."

Meg's mouth fell open. She slowly lowered her finger. "I thought you said you've been employed by my husband for three years."

"We have."

"Is there a reason you didn't testify against the Traxtons?" *Good heavens! If they had, the case might have been closed a long time ago, and Shad wouldn't be missing right now.*

"We tried." Valentina shook her head sadly. "Miguel and I went to the sheriff with our story; but by the time he sent a team of deputies to investigate, the Traxtons had moved the other prisoners. They denied everything, making us look like fools. It has taken your husband years to collect new evidence. This time he's built a case against them they cannot so easily wiggle their way out of."

"Which is why you're worried about my interference."

"Yes." Her housekeeper sounded glum. "But what's done is done. It's in the Lord's hands now." She crossed her chest in the sign of the cross.

Yes, what was done was done, and Meg didn't regret one bit of her part in it. She'd interfere until the end of her days where her husband's safety was concerned. Alas, now that she'd sent her telegram to Jordan Branson, there was truly nothing else she could do. She retired to the attic to wait and pray.

SHAD LAID in the prone beneath the straggly, naked limbs of a Joshua tree. *Have mercy, Lord. I don't know how much longer these men and women can last.* They'd gone too many days and weeks already without proper nourishment during their imprisonment.

It had been a full twelve hours since he and Jason Peck had begun leading the eight Mexican immigrants in the direction of his ranch. The elderly man, whom he'd since learned was named Pablo, had passed out twice and was in dire need of medical care. Rosa Maria, the woman who'd ridden behind him on Diablo, had taken it upon herself to nurse him as best she could. Unfortunately, they'd run out of water hours ago, so there wasn't a whole lot she could do.

The sandstorm had come without warning and taken them by surprise, forcing them to take shelter on a craggy ridge. Alas, no sooner had the sand stopped swirling did the Traxtons and their cronies come looking for them. Thankfully, the wind had erased all trace of their footprints from the sand, but now they were stranded halfway up the side of a mountain. Since they were traveling on foot, there was no way they could outpace the mounted outlaws, and they weren't armed well enough to defend themselves in a fire fight. So they were forced to remain in hiding, growing thirstier, weaker, and more desperate by the hour.

They were lined up like sticks of firewood beneath a copse of Joshua trees.

Peck low-crawled his way to Shad and motioned to borrow his binoculars. He held the lenses up to observe the canyon pass below them. It had been crawling with Traxton operatives all afternoon, making it impossible for them to continue their journey.

"I could mount one of the horses and run a decoy," he said in a low voice. "We need to do something to get these poor folks out of here. Otherwise…"

They both understood all the things that might happen otherwise. Pablo was at the top of their list of concerns.

"Appreciate the offer, but it's too risky right now." Shad accepted the binoculars Peck handed back. "Best to wait until nightfall."

His friend grimaced. "Not sure Pablo has that kind of time."

"I agree, but losing you and exposing the rest of us won't help."

Peck sighed and ran a weary hand over his stubbled jaw. "Lying here and doing nothing is the pits."

"We can pray," Shad suggested mildly. He knew Peck wasn't a man of faith, but prayer was the one thing he'd learned to lean on in times like this. It wasn't the first time he'd found himself running out of options, but God had always been faithful to send help when he needed it the most. And from the way things were shaping up, divine help was Pablo's best hope of surviving the night.

Peck merely grunted in response.

It appeared as if all the praying was up to him. Then again, maybe not. Rosa Maria shifted in the sand and tugged a set of black rosary beads from one of her thick dark braids. Her eyes drifted closed, and her lips moved in silent prayer over them.

Shad was more buoyed by the sight of Rosa Maria praying than by all the pistols and bullets he and Peck possessed between them.

One of his late uncle's favorite scriptures wafted across his mind. It was from the Book of Psalms, chapter eighteen, verse two:

The LORD is my rock, and my fortress, and my deliverer; my God, my strength, in whom I will trust; my buckler, and the horn of my salvation, and my high tower.

Uncle Jon had been as adamant about worship as he was about prayer. He'd warned Shad countless times, *a feller cain't always be askin' fer somethin'. Sometimes he's gotta jes' praise the Lord fer bein' our God.*

While he waited and prayed, his thoughts turned to Meg. He hated leaving her alone yet another night and could only hope she, too, was immersed in prayer right now. He regretted whatever worry his prolonged absence might be causing her, but he gloried in the fact he finally had someone in his life who might actually care whether he made it home at all.

Another dry, hot, sandy hour passed, leaving him and his comrades as parched as a pile of dead leaves.

"Take another look?" Peck motioned for the lenses, and Shad handed them over. "Um, you might want to take a look at this." He hurriedly passed the binoculars back. "Check you're two o'clock."

Shad held up the binoculars and stared transfixed at the sight of the army of men riding over the ridge. They'd not been there a few seconds ago. There were four men riding in front with shotguns pointed in the air, firing over their heads as they flew into the pass. As they drew closer, he could make out the features of Sheriff Chance Otera, the yellow diamond mine owner, Gabe Donovan, and two of his business partners, Levi and Tennyson Barra. A good two dozen or more men flooded the pass behind them.

The Traxton brothers and their men were outnumbered by at least three to one. They quickly shouted a retreat and wheeled their horses around. Otera and his posse thundered after them.

Shad and Jason Peck exchanged a dumbfounded look.

"Come on!" Shad scrambled to a standing position, waving the immigrants to their feet, only to find himself teetering in his boots. He was as lightheaded and off-balance from thirst as a babe learning to walk.

"Whoa there! Whoa!" The shouts of new arrivals and the whinnies of their mounts had Shad, Peck, and the immigrants peering in anxious curiosity down the canyon pass. A pair of wagons rumbled into view, pulled by a team of four horses each. One of the drivers halted, cupped his hands around his mouth, and shouted. "Nicholson, if you can hear me, show yourself. We brought supplies." He waited a moment before repeating his cry "Shadrack Nicholson, if you can hear me..."

Shad stepped out from behind the copse of Joshua trees, waving his hands over his head. His throat and tongue were too parched to shout back. However, Peck and several of the immigrants joined him, waving anything they could get their hands on — their arms, their shirts, and branches from nearby trees.

They were soon surrounded by men bearing water, food, and blankets.

"How did you know we were stranded?" It was the first thing Shad wanted to know after he got a few mouthfuls of water down his throat and recovered his power of speech. "And where to find us?"

One of the younger Barra brothers swaggered into view, hands resting on his pistols. He was either Prescott or Dodge, but Shad wasn't certain which one, only that he possessed the same cocky demeanor as his older brothers.

"Which one of you is Mr. Shadrack Nicholson?" His gaze drifted between him and Jason Peck.

Shad gave him a two-fingered salute. "Who's asking?"

"I am," the impertinent scamp retorted. "I come bearing a message from your wife."

Shad closed his eyes in dizzy exultation. So *she* was the one behind the mounted rescue party! The timing couldn't have been more perfect. He couldn't wait to hold her in his arms again and show her just how much he appreciated her sweet intervention. Without it, things might have turned out quite differently.

CHAPTER 9: THE ANSWER

Miguel returned from town about an hour after his departure, assuring Meg he'd delivered her message to Bram. All that was left for her to do was wait some more and pray some more.

She paced the front porch until dusk, then returned to the attic to stare anxiously out the window. Sleep was going to be impossible tonight. There was no way she could lay her head down on her pillow and close her eyes with Shad still out there in the wilderness unaccounted for.

She lost track of time while she stood there. Eventually, her prayers died on her lips. She was certain she'd uttered every plea of her heart, every hope of her soul. A calm anticipation settled over her. If she truly believed all the things she'd been taught by her family's chaplain, then her prayers had been heard. The next step was expecting an answer.

The shadows deepened, and the moon came out to drench the surrounding mesas and ridges in white light. A low rumble rose in the distance that she felt more than heard. She raced down the attic stairs and second story stairs to throw open the front door.

Black silhouettes of horses and wagons appeared on the horizon and thundered closer.

"Valentina!" she cried. "Miguel! Carlo!"

Hired hands scurried around both sides of the ranch home and assembled on the front lawn. Valentina joined her on the porch, while Miguel and Carlo positioned themselves protectively at the base of the stairs, hands resting on their weapons.

"Our prayers are answered," Valentina breathed. "It's Prescott Barra."

"Who?" Meg hissed.

"A neighbor," she explained and added belatedly. "Of sorts."

As it turned out, their neighbor *of sorts* had a special delivery. When he halted his wagon, a sunburnt but exultant Shad Nicholson leaped down and staggered in their direction.

With a small scream of joy, Meg raced down the porch stairs and straight into his arms. "You came back to me," she exclaimed. "Just like you said you would."

He buried his face in her neck and held her tightly as if he never intended to let her go. "Thank you." His voice was hoarse and weary. "If you hadn't sent help when you did, I'm not certain I would have been able to keep my word to you after all."

"All I did was ask," she confessed when he raised his head. She pointed upwards. "I did nothing on my own but wait and pray. I think we both know where your help really came from."

"Oh, Meg!" He shook his head at her and crooned tenderly, "What did I ever do to deserve such a treasure? You're so beautiful and talented and wise!"

She made a snorting sound. "Not in the realm of culinary arts, I'm afraid. You've not been around much to witness my failures in the kitchen, but I've discovered it's actually possible to burn water."

He broke into a guffaw that made heads turn in their direction. "Say it isn't so, darling!"

"Oh, it's so." Her heart melted at the sound of the endearment on his lips. "Just ask the ranch hands. Thankfully, Carlo came to my rescue after I let the horrid Tandy go. He's proven himself to be quite a wizard with a spatula. I wouldn't have survived without his assistance."

"His assistance, eh?" Her husband's grin widened.

She snickered and rested her head on his shoulder. "Indeed. If you want your dinners to be edible, you might wish to consider lending me his services in the kitchen for the foreseeable future." She tipped her face up to his, caressing his cheek. "At least until I learn how to quit burning water."

"I think that can be arranged." He nuzzled her lips. "I've a good many other ideas in mind for how to best employ your talents."

"You do?" She could hardly put two lucid thoughts together with the warmth of his mouth brushing against hers.

"Yes, indeed." He swooped in for a much longer, more satisfying kiss before continuing. "As it happens, I'm traveling with eight guests who could desperately use your sweet brand of interference in their lives." He kissed her again before raising his head and slowly spinning her around.

"I do *not* interfere. I simply…interject myself where I'm needed and make the necessary adjustments," she assured with a haughty tilt to her chin.

"Exactly." His chuckle was low and husky in her ear. "Behold a group who will be grateful for every adjustment you make to their pitiful existence."

They surveyed the ragtag group of Mexican fugitives together, and Meg drew in a shuddering breath of sympathy.

"Oh, Shad! You did it! You got to them in time."

"With Peck's help."

Her busy mind raced over all the things that would need to be done to get them settled and comfortable. "They need baths, clothing, and shoes. Plus they'll need regular meals to put some color back in their cheeks. And a place to sleep with plenty of beds, blankets, and pillows." Her arms tightened around Shad's middle as she warmed to the task at hand. "I'm not certain we possess enough cottages to house them all, or if the ones we have will be big enough in the long run. Boys need room to stretch and grow, you know."

Shad kissed her earlobe. "What are you suggesting, wife?"

A giggle escaped her. "I'm not certain Miguel has forgiven me yet for my first construction project. Do you think he'll be willing to commence another one so soon?"

"Perhaps if we hire a crew from Hope's Landing to assist him, he won't fuss too loudly."

She squealed and stood on tiptoe to wrap her arms around his neck. "Perhaps we shouldn't give away or burn my fortune after all. Methinks we could put it to much better use hiring more workers and building more cottages."

"On that we agree." He lifted her from her feet and swung her in a circle. "See? I warned you it might take a little time to set you free from the trappings of wealth, but some things are worth waiting for."

"Some things are most definitely worth waiting for," she breathed as he set her back on her feet.

His ranch and all the people dwelling there, the new life they were building together, this overwhelming sense of peace and contentment... She gazed around the moonlit lawn at all the happy chaos taking place around them. This was exactly what her heart had been waiting for.

EPILOGUE

Eight months later

The kick inside Meg's belly made her lay down the small blanket she was knitting to rub a hand down her blooming midsection. "Heavens, but you're an energetic little poppet!" she whispered. Lately, she'd found herself speaking to her unborn child aloud.

Miss Hiss rose from the step where she'd been sunning and arched her back with a short yowl of contentment. Then she loped across the porch to Meg's rocker to rub her head against her mistress's shoe. Ever since she'd start increasing, the cat had taken to following her around like a faithful little shadow.

A childish shriek of delight around the corner was followed by muffled laughter as one of the immigrant boys found the other in their endless game of hide-and-seek across the ranch grounds.

Meg stood and twisted from one side to the other to dispel a cramp. She was finding it more and more difficult to be comfortable for long, whether sitting or standing. The babe was growing so quickly and stretching her to the point of feeling like she was surely going to pop. "Hurry up, little one." She brushed a hand across her belly again, already so much in love with the tiny little human she had yet to lay eyes on. She couldn't wait to hold him for the very first time. "Your papa is coming home any day now. Then everything will be in tip-top shape for your grand entrance into the world."

Shad had been gone a week, swearing it was his last absence before their child's arrival. She missed him more than she dared to admit and prayed he would be able to keep his word this time. He'd spent the last eight months unearthing the final pockets of fugitives the Traxtons had stashed throughout the countryside. Some he'd been able to return to anxiously awaiting family members; others he'd brought home to his wife to nurse back to health. He'd received a tip a few weeks ago about a final group of fugitives hiding in the canyons in desperate need of nourishment and supplies.

Something in her chest told her today would be the day he would return. It was the sole reason she was sitting on the porch. Valentina had come to check on her a dozen times, and Carlo had served her both breakfast and lunch out here; but she refused to give up her vigil.

Just over the rise beyond the front lawn, she glimpsed the silhouette of a man on horseback. Shad's private posse of soldiers were ever on patrol. Day and night, they circled the ranch and its growing rows of shacks that housed their immigrant workers.

Meg was very happy with the progress Miguel and his hired team of construction workers had made throughout the summer. He'd transformed Shad's ranch into a community of its own. They possessed pastures of farm animals, fields of crops, three enormous hothouses full of more succulent plants, and an able-bodied crew to manage it all.

Meg and Valentina had become fast friends with Rosa Maria, her elderly mother, and her cousin, Celia. As it turned out, Rosa Maria and her mother were skilled weavers. Shortly after their arrival, they'd begun churning out lambs wool socks, blankets, and various clothing items. This had led to Shad opening a boutique for them on the road leading into town. They sold their woven products there, insisting Meg and Valentina display their paintings alongside their brightly dyed wares.

Celia, on the other hand, proved to have a gifted green thumb. Her unusual and vivid shades of hothouse roses were the talk of the town. They were also in constant demand at weddings, funerals, town picnics, church services, and other events.

"Meg, won't you come inside?" Valentina sighed from the doorway of her ranch home. "You've been outside all day." She clutched one of Rosa Maria's beautiful, hand-woven blankets.

Meg's fingers curled around the porch railing. "I'd rather stay here a little longer." Waiting for and worrying about Shad never got easier, but it was becoming more of a normal part of her existence. She was the wife of a federal marshal, and certain responsibilities came along with it.

"He has Salvador with him," her friend reminded. She glided in her typical silent manner across the porch to drape the blanket around Meg's shoulders. Salvador was one of the ex-*Rurales* police Shad had hired to protect Meg. Somehow, he and his two companions had never gotten around to leaving the Nicholsons' employ and were now a permanent fixture in their lives.

"I know." Meg drew a deep breath and slowly let it out. She didn't mind the presence of the ex-patriots nearly as much as she had in the beginning. Salvador, Mateo, and Iker were practically family now — three more men for her to feed, clothe, house, and look after, which delighted her to no end. Quite honestly, she was almost as anxious to see Salvador return home safely as she was to see her own husband.

Valentina reached for her hand. "I caught Rosa Maria sighing over Celia's roses this morning. I suspect it might have something to do with Salvador's pending return."

Meg smiled. "So that's the way the wind blows."

"Like a sweet summer storm," her friend chuckled. "It's a good thing Miguel has gotten started on that chapel you asked him to build."

In the distance, a dust cloud billowed.

"It's them," Meg breathed, gripping Valentina's hand tighter.

Together, the women watched the men in the dust cloud take shape. As they rode nearer, it became apparent there were more than two men approaching — quite a few more, in fact. Women and children, too.

"What in the world?" Meg squinted for a better look as ranch hands came pouring across the front lawn. They stationed themselves protectively between the two women on the porch and the approaching riders.

"It's Shad!" she cried joyfully. Her husband was finally home! That was all that mattered. She pushed away from the railing, preparing to dash down the stairs, but Valentina detained her by keeping a grip on her hand.

"Wait," she insisted. "We don't yet know who he has with him. Best to be cautious."

The men in the yard fell silent as Shad and Salvador approached with their companions.

"Oh-h-h!" Meg couldn't believe what she was seeing. The fugitives Shad had unearthed this time weren't Mexican as she'd anticipated; they were Chinese! She counted four men of indeterminate ages, two exotic looking young women, and three small children that resembled dolls.

"I'll see to them," Valentina said quickly. "Rosa Maria and Celia will help me. You may come check on them later. But first, I believe someone has come to check on you."

Shad rode across the lawn, seeking out Meg with his eyes. The moment his gaze lighted on hers, he leaped from his horse, not waiting for the creature to come to a complete halt. He ran in her direction. This time, Valentina didn't stop her when she flew down the porch stairs to greet him.

He slowed his stride, tossed his Stetson aside, and caught her in a velvety hold.

"I've missed you," he growled against her mouth.

"I missed you more." She returned his hungry kisses, every last worry of the past week sliding to the ground and shattering at their feet.

"I highly doubt it." He plunged a hand in her curls and canted her head to give him better access, slanting his mouth over hers.

Their babe gave a hearty kick against his gut, making him draw back to survey her anxiously. "That was a rather powerful one. Are you alright, sweetheart?"

"Yes. He's a lively little fellow. I've hardly gotten a wink of sleep since you've been gone," she teased in a faux complaining voice, though their son's antics gave her nothing but joy.

"You're still so certain it's a boy?" Shad's brown eyes softened in wonder.

"I am, which brings us to the all-important topic of names." She drummed her fingers idly on the shoulder of his leather vest. "I've had a lot of time this week to think about it. If you've no objections to the idea, I'd like to name him after the two men in the world I love the most." Or loved. Past tense. One of them was no longer with her.

Shad's brows rose, and he barely seemed to be breathing as he awaited her next words.

"Herman Shadrack." She anxiously watched for his reaction. He knew she'd never been close with her father, but that didn't change the fact she'd always loved him.

He drew a callused finger down her cheek. "I like the name. I also like hearing that you love me. You never said the words before." His voice shook a little.

She caught her lower lip between her teeth. "You didn't know I love you?" How was that possible? He was her first thought when she awoke every morning and her last thought before she closed her eyes each night. She was carrying his babe, for crying out loud!

"I've been hoping, but I wasn't certain until now." He cuddled her closer. "It's been hard waiting. I wanted so badly to ask, but I didn't want to rush my fences. Those feelings take time to develop. Not with me, as it turns out, but..."

"Not with you, eh?" She stood on tiptoe to bring them nose to nose. "If you've been holding out on me, Marshal Nicholson," she threatened.

"Have pity on a man, will you?" He brushed his lips tenderly against hers. "I've been privately drowning in love for months over a tiny slip of a woman I'm not half worthy of."

"Why, Shad!" His words both shocked and humbled her. She'd never dreamt that hearing her declaration of love would mean so much to him. "Of course, I love you. I think I've loved you since the moment I stepped off the train, and I haven't the slightest notion what you mean about not being worthy of me. Why, I've spent the last eight months trying to prove myself worthy of *you!*"

Her husband's eyes were suspiciously bright as he

scooped her up in his arms and carried inside their home without a backwards glance.

"What about our new arrivals?" The look in his eyes was making her insides melt.

"They're in good hands," he assured roughly. "And right now, you're in mine."

Happiness flooded Meg as she clung to him. There was nowhere else on earth she'd rather be than in the arms of the man she loved.

Thank you for reading
MISUNDERSTOOD MEG!
I hope you love Meg & Shad's story. The adventures of the next Gallant Rescuer will continue in
Mail Order Brides Rescue Series #5:
Dare-Devil Daisy

A DEBUTANTE WANTING **to marry quickly, a rough and tough cowboy on the hunt for a wife, and neither are being completely honest about their intentions...**

To the world, Daisy Danvers is a spoiled young debutante from Boston who always gets what she wants. But she has secrets — big, festering secrets she doesn't want her best friend, Meg Nicholson, to find out. All she needs from Meg is a promise to help her find the perfect husband the moment she steps off the train in Headstone, Arizona. Her very life may depend upon it.

She never dreamed her troubles would follow her out west, and a whole posse of armed robbers would be waiting for her when she disembarked. She also never dreamed a cocky cowboy would sweep her away to safety on his horse.

It's way too bad the devilishly handsome Prescott Barra

claims he's already affianced to another woman, because he's everything she's been looking for in a husband. He's brave and fearless with a streak of adventure as wide as the canyons they're riding through. When she discovers he has a secret or two of his own, she begins to hope that maybe — just maybe — their secrets will lead them to each other.

I hope you loved
MISUNDERSTOOD MEG!
Please leave a review.
Then keep turning the page for a sneak peek at our next Gallant Rescuer in
Dare-Devil Daisy

Much love,
Jovie

SNEAK PREVIEW: DARE-DEVIL DAISY

*P*rescott Barra was desperately weary of his two older brothers, Levi and Tennyson, strutting around like lords of the manor on the homestead they jointly owned. So they'd both managed to wed themselves to uppity women from the east? Tennyson had tied the knot with a lovely debutant named Callie, and Levi was head over heels with his lawyer wife named Felicity.

It's not that he had anything against either woman; they both seemed nice enough. It's just that he was fresh out of temper with the way Levi and Tennyson had persisted in trying to manage the lives of their two younger brothers ever since they'd gotten hitched — as if becoming married men had somehow given them the right to stick their noses in other folks' business.

They could manage Dodge all they wanted; he was barely seventeen and still in school; but he needed to find a way to set the record straight about his own life. He was pushing twenty, was no longer in school, and didn't require older brothers trying to double as nursemaids.

For the fifth straight week in a row, he nosed his horse in the direction of the Nicholson ranch. There wasn't another rodeo scheduled for him to ride in for a good two weeks, so he was bored out of his mind. And though he held a profitable percentage in the yellow diamond mine at Hope's Landing, it seemed he wasn't much cut out for administration. One of his primary responsibilities was training new hires, but it would be days before they ushered in their next round of recruits.

Fortunately, his other responsibility was overseeing their various construction projects. There weren't any current buildings being raised at Hope's Landing, but there sure were plenty of them being build at the Nicholson ranch. Thankfully, Gabe and Hannah Donovan had seen fit to subcontract out his services with them.

Shad Nicholson was their closest neighbor and a federal marshal to boot. Prescott had liked the fellow ever since he'd gone toe to toe with the diabolical Traxtons and their human trafficking cronies. He was proud of the fact he'd ridden with the posse that the man's wife, Meg, had summoned during their final showdown against the Traxtons. Thanks to her quick thinking, the desperadoes were behind bars, and her husband was still alive.

Maybe it was because Shad Nicholson didn't stand half a foot above the rest of humanity like the tall, dark, and rugged Barra brothers. Or maybe it was because Shad had nothing to prove like the social climbing older Barras who seemed anxious to leave behind their wild oats reputation after practically raising themselves. All Prescott knew was that he was comfortable working around the marshal. Most importantly, he treated him like a man instead of a boy.

He'd be lying to himself, though, if he claimed Shad's regard was the only reason he kept coming to work at the Nicholson's ranch. The truth was, he wasn't just bored; he was lonely. And maybe just a wee bit envious of the happiness his older brothers had found with their new wives…

With a grunt of sheer self-disgust, he dismounted his horse at the large double doors of the Nicholson's main barn. Miguel, Shad's best friend, was waiting for him, coppery arms crossed. From what he gathered, the man more or less ran the place during Shad's many extended absences as a lawman. He oversaw the ranch hands and the day-to-day operations of the ranch itself, while his wife, Valentina, seemed to be in charge of the household staff and the various endeavors of the womenfolk who helped harvest the crops, wove woolen cloth, and ran a thriving boutique down the road

"You are late, *amigo*." Miguel seemed to have a permanent scowl painted across his sunburnt features.

Prescott snorted. He didn't report to Miguel, nor did he have a set arrival time. "How's the chapel coming along?" It was their latest construction project. For reasons Miguel didn't explain, he seemed anxious to finish it within the week.

"Your men paint today." His English was broken, but it was improving after several months of working with Prescott's crew.

Prescott nodded. "I'll go check on their progress for myself." He'd tasked them to arrive at sun-up to maximize their use of daylight hours. It was best to get all the exterior finish work done while the weather was holding. One never knew when a sandstorm would blow through and delay their efforts for days.

"*No, amigo. Señorita* Meg must see you first." He unfolded his arms, reached for the reins of Prescott's horse, and hitched one thumb towards the main ranch house.

Prescott's brows rose. The stunning Meg Nicholson wanted to speak with him? Whatever for? He had work to do

— real work — that did not include sipping tea with someone else's new wife no matter how easy she was on the eyes.

A harried glance back at Miguel proved the man was already leading his horse away to be brushed down and watered. *Ah, so be it!* With a growl of irritation, he stomped towards the ranch house. He'd hear whatever the princess of the house had to say, wave away her blasted tea, and be on his way to the construction site in no time.

Figuring it was most proper to knock at the front door instead of the back, he strode around the enormous, wrap-around porch. His steps slowed. Meg Nicholson was sitting in a rocker on the front porch with an expectant expression and a belly beneath her emerald gown that looked ready to burst.

Her hazel eyes lit, and she stood.

"Please." He increased his stride, hurrying in her direction with his hands upraised. "Do not stand on my account. A woman in your condition…" He let his words dwindle, realizing he knew exactly nothing about women in her condition.

She laughed merrily and sat, motioning him to take a seat in the rocker next to hers.

He arched one brow at her, took the porch stairs two at a time, and lounged back against the railing. He might have answered her royal summons, but there was no way he would be caught dead by any passers-by rocking like some wizened old granny on her front porch.

"La, but you're so tall you're making my neck hurt," she teased with a delicious little feminine chuckle.

He sat, feeling foolish, and prayed there would be no witnesses to the fact he'd traded in his horse for a rocker this morning.

Meg's smile disappeared. "I am grateful you were willing

to take the time to meet with me. I declare, with Shad constantly dashing out of town, I hardly knew who else to turn to."

She had his full attention now. Whatever she wanted to discuss sounded dreadfully serious. "Anything," he assured. His own regard for Shad bordered on idol worship, not that anyone needed to know that foolish fact. He'd do just about anything to help the man in his absence.

"Ah." Meg shook her head, sending her long, blonde corkscrew curls dancing. "I'm forgetting my manners. Would you care for some tea? Valentina is brewing a fresh pot."

So help me, no! He waved his hand to turn down the frivolous offer to tip teacups with her and hoped he managed to hide his grimace.

"In that case," she sighed. "Back to the troublesome matter at hand." She unfolded a letter he'd not noticed she was holding until just this moment, scanned its contents, and closed her eyes as if in distress.

"What is it, madame?" He leaned forward anxiously. "If you're in any sort of trouble…" He'd move heaven or hell to make whatever needed to be made right for Shad's wife.

"I am not in trouble." She opened her eyelids to reveal a gaze drenched in concern. "But a dear friend is."

"Oh?" He rested his elbows on his knees, waiting for her to continue.

"Technically, I don't know her half as well as I'd like. My father never permitted us much time together. He was too fearful for my safety, but I suppose she was as close to a best friend as a girl in my shoes was allowed to have while growing up. At any rate, we've continued to correspond with each other since my journey to Arizona."

Prescott wasn't certain where this strange conversation was leading nor what it could possibly have to do with him, but he tried to hide his impatience to be on his way. His respect for Shad Nicholson demanded it.

"Alas, the sweet thing has convinced herself I'm on some glorious adventure in the wild west, and she cannot wait to join me here." Her voice rose on a note of pure distress.

For the life of him, Prescott couldn't see what was so bad about that.

"As a mail-order bride!" she wailed, clasping the much-rumpled letter to her chest.

Ah! He hid a chuckle behind a cough. He was beginning to see the problem.

"So what I need you to do, what I am absolutely begging you to consider, is riding into Headstone — today, if possible — to send an urgent telegram to the Boomtown Mail Order Brides Company." She gave a dramatic pause and seemed to be struggling to catch her breath.

"And tell them what exactly?" he prodded, feeling the first stirrings of alarm beneath his vest.

"You must save her from whatever dusty, dime-a-dozen cowboy they might try to pair her with and agree to be her groom, of course."

His jaw dropped so far, he was surprised he didn't feel the porch planks bump his chin.

"She has a history of getting herself into scrapes, and I am convinced she has no idea what she's getting herself into this time." Meg fanned her face with the letter. "Furthermore, I have no doubt she will realize her mistake within twenty-four hours after her arrival and purchase a ticket on the next train back to Boston." There was a curious break to her voice. "All I'm asking is that you be the one to greet her at the train station and pose as her prospective groom. There is no one else I trust with the task. No one else whom I can guarantee will behave like a true gentleman and send her back to Boston with her virtue intact."

Prescott slowly straightened in his rocking chair and leaned back heavily against the whitewashed slats. *Jumping Jehoshaphat!* Of all the favors he'd speculated might be asked of him after he woke this morning, getting married — or pretending to — was not one of them. Not even close! He rubbed a hand over his stubbled jaw, wondering what his work crew must be thinking of his prolonged absence.

"Please, Prescott." Meg's beseeching voice tugged him back to the present. "You're my only hope of saving this friend from utter ruin."

He let out a frustrated whoosh of air. "Why me?" He spread his calloused hands. She had a ranch full of male worker bees. Why not fancy up one of them in a suit and tie and have them go pose as this capricious young woman's groom?

"Because you're the only one I trust with a matter so delicate." She studied him shrewdly. "No doubt you're wondering why I do not ask the nearest farm hand."

"Well, yes." His tone was dry.

"For one thing, a good number of them can barely speak English. For another thing, they do not possess your social graces."

A snort escaped him. "Surely you've mistaken me with someone else." He stood, unable to contain his impatience any longer. He'd been raised by brothers whose efforts hadn't always been square on the right side of the law, and he was physically scarred from years of bull riding on the rodeo circuit. He was not the debonair man Meg Nicholson seemed to think he was. The sooner he disabused her of the notion he might make a proper groom for her friend, the better for both of them. And the better for her friend, as well.

"Maybe I have." Her voice turned bitter. "Because I certainly never once mistook you for a coward."

He pivoted in his well-worn boot heels to face her, unable to believe what he was hearing.

"She's an innocent young woman who deserves my protection," she snapped. "And yours, I'd hoped, considering I am in no condition to…" She waved her hands at her blossoming belly. "Well, look at me! I'm utterly useless in this state."

Prescott gnashed his teeth, feeling as if he was being wholly maneuvered by events outside his control. He could hardly believe it when he heard his own voice answer. "Fine. I'll send that blasted telegram, and greet your little friend at the train depot." No one was going to call him a coward and get away with it.

The storm swirling across Meg's features cleared. She stood and held out both hands to him. "You dear, dear man! I am so happy you've agreed to help me."

That made one them. He was fairly certain it was the most foolish thing he'd ever been asked to do.

"I'll be sure to tell Shad how kind you were to me in his absence."

Right. He was only doing this to help out a man he respected. Or at least the friend of a wife of a man he respected… Which was the same thing, wasn't it? His brain hurt just thinking about it.

"What is her name?" he asked abruptly. He at least deserved to know the name of the chit he was going to be saddled with for a few days.

"Daisy." Meg beamed at him. "Daisy Danvers, though some folks like to call her Dare-Devil Daisy."

Blast it all! Helping Daisy sounded like a pack of trouble. Then again, he was a Barra brother. Trouble followed him everywhere he went. Trouble was his middle name.

I hope you enjoyed the first chapter of
Mail Order Brides Rescue Series #5:
Dare-Devil Daisy.

This complete 12-book series is available now in eBook, paperback, and Kindle Unlimited on Amazon.

Read them all!
Hot-Tempered Hannah
Cold-Feet Callie
Fiery Felicity
Misunderstood Meg
Dare-Devil Daisy
Outrageous Olivia
Jinglebell Jane
Absentminded Amelia
Bookish Belinda
Tenacious Trudy
Meddlesome Madge
Mismatched MaryAnne
MOB Rescue Series Box Set Books 1-4
MOB Rescue Series Box Set Books 5-8
MOB Rescue Series Box Set Books 9-12

Much love,
Jovie

GET A FREE BOOK!

Join my mailing list to be the first to know about new releases, free books, special discount prices, Bonus Content, and giveaways.

https://BookHip.com/GNVABPD

NOTE FROM JOVIE

Guess what? I have some Bonus Content for you. Read a little more about the swoony cowboy heroes in my books by signing up for my mailing list.

There will be a special Bonus Content chapter for each new

book I write, just for my subscribers. Plus, you get a FREE book just for signing up!

Thank you for reading and loving my books.

JOIN CUPPA JO READERS!

If you're on Facebook, you're invited to join my group, Cuppa Jo Readers. Saddle up for some fun reader games and giveaways + book chats about my sweet and swoon-worthy cowboy book heroes!

https://www.facebook.com/groups/CuppaJoReaders

SNEAK PREVIEW: LAWFULLY WITNESSED

March, 1862

"We're at war, Papa. It's only a matter of time before the fighting reaches Atlanta."

Twenty-year-old Anna Kate cringed at the sound of angry male voices downstairs. The war might as well be taking place in their living room from the number of family arguments it had sparked lately. However, her brothers were right. The Monroe family could not afford to hide their heads in the sand any longer. Trouble was coming their way, whether they were ready or not.

She stood silently in front of the dressing mirror in her second-story bedchamber as she fluffed her long blonde hair enticingly around her shoulders. Staring critically at her pink silk gown with its ruffled chiffon overlay, she wished more than anything there was a party she could wear it to this evening. Like most folks, she agreed the war was a horrible thing and sorely wished it would go away, but that didn't keep her from appreciating how nice the newest batch of soldier recruits looked in their uniforms. It made her heart flutter just thinking about all those royal blue trousers and light gray jackets. The scarlet trim edging them and rows of shiny brass buttons brought to mind no end of breathtaking acts of bravery and heroism.

She indulged in a gusty sigh of self-pity, not wanting to dwell on the battles to come. At the moment, she was wallowing in a different sort of melancholy, because the war had stolen more than her family's peace. It had also utterly destroyed the all-important social season that every southern belle of marriageable age looked forward to.

There would be no parties for her this year — no teas, picnics, musicales, or holiday gatherings. With rumors of military skirmishes popping up all over the state of Georgia, Papa wasn't willing to let her out of his sight these days. He wouldn't even let her go on horseback rides or walks any longer. She'd all but become a prisoner in their home. If something didn't change soon, she was going to spiral into utter madness! A girl could only paint so many watercolors or practice so many hours on the pianoforte. She desperately needed something more to do or, better yet, some place else to go.

Lost in contemplation, she nibbled on her lower lip as she glided to her bedchamber door. Turning the knob and pushing it open, she paused when a knock sounded on the front door. *Dear heavens, let it be the milk man. Or a neighbor.* Not someone bearing any more bad news.

She glided from her room to peer over the balcony railing to the grand foyer below. Their butler of many years, Frederick, materialized as silently as a ghost to answer the door. He was an unsmiling, middle-aged man with his hair slicked back by too much pomade. She wrinkled her nose at the somber black suit he persisted in wearing, despite her many attempts over the years to elevate his wardrobe to something less funereal. A pin-striped waistcoat, perhaps, or even a vest. Something with a dash of color, for pity's sake.

After a hushed exchange of words with someone she could not see from her vantage point, she observed him accepting a small white envelope on the silver tray he always carried with him.

He firmly shut the front door, performed a perfect pivot on the heels of his perfectly shined shoes, and squarely met her gaze as if he'd already known she was standing there. Since she was a small child, she'd always wondered if he had eyes in the back of his head, a trait she found most irritating.

"It is a letter, Miss Anna Kate," he announced in a smooth, well-modulated voice that she sorely doubted even the war could frazzle. "For you."

"For me?" Her flagging spirits perked at the thought of receiving news from out of town. So often these days, the mail was delayed or failed to run at all. "How wonderful!" She moved down the stairs, as fast as a proper lady was allowed, to whisk the precious envelope from his tray.

"Ahem," he said quietly as she wordlessly spun away from him.

"Thank you, Frederick." Knowing the man was as curious as she was about the letter, though far too hoity-toity to ask any questions, it delighted her to no end to dismiss him with a flutter of her fingers. Whoever had written her and whatever news they had to impart was for her eyes alone.

The dinner hour was fast approaching, so she didn't return to her bedchamber. Instead, she slipped inside the front parlor and cozied herself in a windowed alcove. Normally, dinner time was her favorite time of day — the *only* time of day, really, that she could pretend the Monroes were still one big happy family. But her menfolk seemed bent on ruining that little fantasy of hers this evening. She tried to block out their bellowing as she turned the envelope over to see how it was addressed.

Why, it was from Winifred Monroe, her father's only sister! She was an eccentric woman several years his senior, a confirmed spinster who'd thumbed her nose at their southern roots and moved west over a decade earlier.

Aunt Win! Though most of the family considered her an oddball, Anna Kate had always enjoyed her infrequent visits during holidays, funerals, and such. Her Aunt Winifred was an outspoken woman with an infectious laugh, one of those rare creatures who wasn't afraid to speak her mind.

Anna Kate's father's voice rose in agitation from the other end of the hallway, making her pause before opening the letter. "I don't believe in shirking one's duties, son. However, we have a rail and supply center to keep running downtown. I know it may not seem as glorious as shouldering a rifle, but who do you think gets those rifles to where they're going?" He sounded very much the part of Jack Monroe, or Jack Senior as his closest friends and associates liked to call him, the proud owner of a line of bustling shipping yards and warehouses. From what she understood, he more or less cornered the market on storage and shipping in the greater Atlanta area, which served as the nerve center for their region. It meant her family was wealthy — vastly wealthy in ways that even the war itself couldn't diminish. In fact, Monroe Industries had been booming with business ever since the wheels of the war machine started turning.

"Profits, you mean!" her oldest brother, Jackson, growled. "That's all you've ever cared about, isn't it? The bottom line and nothing else."

Anna Kate rolled her eyes and tried to block out their angry voices. They'd been going at each other's throats like rabid dogs since daybreak. It was the same old argument they'd been having ever since the war began.

Jackson was a Union sympathizer and wanted their family to pack up and flee to their vacation home in the Blue Ridge Mountains, whereas Jack Senior had no intention of abandoning their family business.

"I know it's not as exciting as following the drum, and it may not feel as adventurous as hightailing it to the mountains, son, but this is our home," her father's voice rumbled. "We work and we carry on, the same way as every other Monroe has been doing for generations."

Jackson made a growling sound that traveled menacingly down the hallway and across the parlor to the velvet divan where Anna Kate was perched. "And when the Confederacy finally ratifies that Conscription Bill they've been yammering on and on about? Then what, Papa?" There was a pointed silence, during which she could envision the glare he was giving Jack Senior. "I reckon you'll just quietly keep running our rail and supply business when they come to cart Will, Grady, and myself off to Heaven only knows where?"

Conscription! Allowing the letter to drop unopened into her lap, Anna Kate clapped a hand over her mouth. She couldn't bear the thought of watching Jackson being drafted and taken away from her, much less Will and Grady. Their younger brothers were but teens! Surely, the Confederacy would consider them a mite young for donning a uniform and picking up a rifle.

Snatching up the letter from Aunt Win, she pushed aside the heavy brocade curtains separating the alcove from the rest of the parlor. "Papa!" she gasped. Throwing all decorum aside, she lifted her skirts and ran down the wide tiled hall. "Papa!" She rounded the corner and skidded to a halt in the arched doorway leading to the library.

Two pairs of eyes stared back, as blue as her own. Jack Senior was standing by the mantle in one of his dark business suits. The evening sunlight pouring through the picture window illuminated the navy wool and silk weave of the fabric and the custom tailored stitches that held it together.

"Well, there's my favorite southern belle." An indulgent smile tugged the corners of her father's mouth, and the tiny lines at the edges of his eyes became more pronounced. "I trust you had an enjoyable afternoon, sugar?"

"Don't, Papa," she choked. Couldn't he see she was in no frame of mind to engage in small talk about her painting and embroidery projects? "I couldn't help overhearing what you said about the Conscription Bill." Her heart pounded with trepidation as she faced her oldest brother, a hand fisting her skirts in agitation. "Is it true, Jackson? Are they truly getting close to passing it?"

He stood across the room from her with his feet firmly planted on the Persian rug beside the pianoforte, arms crossed and jaw clenched in stubbornness. "I believe it is both likely and imminent," he affirmed. The chill in his voice and stance were directed at their father, not her.

"Then what are we going to do?" Her voice dropped to a fearful whisper. They'd lost their mother to a fever a few years earlier. Anna Kate couldn't bear the thought of losing anyone else she loved.

"My concern, exactly!" Jackson declared harshly. "What are we going to do, Papa? And whatever it is, we'd best do it soon before the choice is taken out of our hands."

Jack Senior grew very still, and his eyes took on an icy cast that Anna Kate had never seen before. "This *is* my choice, son. That's what I've been trying to tell you all along. If you're looking for my blessing to do otherwise, I'll give it and gladly, but this is where I'll be staying."

Dread filled Anna Kate's chest. She was sick of the war and beyond weary of the way it was dividing her beloved family.

Jackson slowly uncurled his arms to fist his hands at his

sides. "That's it?" He sounded shocked and incredulous. "You're throwing your support to the plantation owners? Why?" He looked incensed. "Slavery is wrong, Papa, and you know it. You've admitted it in so many words to me, yourself."

His father angrily batted the air with his hand. "Bah! I'll never own a slave, and I've been doing everything in my power to end such a morally repugnant practice for years. But the war is about more than that, son. It's about fighting to defend what's ours. Our families, our homes, our land, and our businesses." His tone grew tighter. "If you've got your stubborn head set on having an answer from me today, then you'll have it, by George! This is where I'm taking my stand yesterday, today, and tomorrow." He pointed to the floor. "Running Monroe Industries is my contribution to the cause of freedom, just like it was my father's contribution and my grandfather's contribution before that."

Anna Kate's agonized gaze met her brother's furious one. No more words were required. After months of Jackson's goading, Papa was finally choosing a side. He'd been born a southern man, and he would die a southern man.

She dropped her head and stared blindly at the letter in her hand as a deathly silence settled around them.

"Is that a letter, sugar?" her father inquired after a pregnant pause.

She nodded mutely, not yet able to meet his gaze. "It is from Aunt Win." She held it out to him without looking up.

"It's addressed to you, sweetheart," he noted in a mild voice. "Why don't you open it and read it to us?" Waving at her to join him, he walked around the velvet sofa, each footstep echoing with dreaded finality against the hardwood floor.

She sat on the cushion beside him and mechanically tore open the envelope. The scent of her aunt's favorite lavender water assailed her nose as she untucked the letter and opened it.

> *My dearest niece,*
>
> *I hope this letter finds you in better health than me. Alas, the doctor says my rheumatism is getting worse and has advised me to seek out a companion. My man of business handles most of the day-to-day work for the railroad spur. However, my duties continue to require an overwhelming amount of correspondence. Naturally, with your lovely penmanship, your name was the first that came to mind, sweet girl. I do not know the odds of that doting father of yours being willing to part with you for any length of time, but I'll gladly keep you in Briar Gate as long as he can spare you. At the very least, it will give you a break from the horrid war...*

Anna Kate hastily skimmed the rest of her aunt's letter, right down to the part where she sent her love to them all. "I should go," she announced to no one in particular.

As much as she hated the idea of being away for an extended period from her father and brothers, her aunt was right. She sorely needed a break, but not from the war. She needed a break from the constant duel of words taking place in her own home, and she didn't mind in the least that her visit to Texas would require some industry on her part. Penning letters for her aunt would give her something meaningful to do. Something that mattered.

"I agree, my dear," her father noted in such a gentle voice that it made Anna Kate's eyes sting with tears. She'd expected his vehement opposition to the idea.

"You're sending me away," she muttered, blinking rapidly to hold the sting of moisture in her eyes at bay.

"That I am," he sighed, moving off the couch to crouch down in front of her. "Jackson has the right of it, love. I should have sent you to a safer place months ago." He reached for her hand and cradled it between his two strong, sturdy ones. "I've been selfish in keeping you here like a caged animal. You were meant to fly free, little bird." He squeezed her hand.

She shook her head fiercely. She might not always agree with his decisions, but selfishness was not what motivated him. It was love. "No, Papa, I—"

"Let me finish," he begged in a voice rough with emotion. "I cannot stomach the thought of parting with you, Will, and Grady, but that is exactly what I must do. It is the only way I can ensure you will remain safe, considering what is coming." He drew an uneven breath.

The stinging behind her eyelids grew worse. "But Papa—"

"No buts, sugar. I promised your mama this was exactly what I would do when the time came."

She tasted bitterness. He was referring to the war again, always the dratted war! "And Jackson?" The first tear escaped and slid down her cheek as she whipped her head up to meet her brother's troubled gaze. He was more opposed to the war than anyone she knew, yet she could already read his decision. It was written across his features and mirrored in his clear blue eyes. He did not intend to accompany her and their younger brothers to Texas.

He nodded to affirm her fear. "I'll stay with Papa."

"Oh, Jackson!" She didn't know what else to say.

"My place is with him, Anna Kate. War or no war, I'll not be leaving him alone."

She stood, sobbing silently at the finality in his voice. When Jackson got like this, she knew there was no changing his mind. He could be as stubborn as Papa sometimes.

"I'll stay, too," she choked. Her earlier woes about the lack of parties in town seemed awfully petty now. There were far bigger things at stake. If Jackson could sacrifice the things he'd rather be doing, then so could she.

"No, sugar. You will not." Papa rose to stand before her. "Jackson is right. You and your younger brothers need to head to safer ground." When he gathered her in his arms, she knew with sudden certainty that one rift in their family had been mended at long last. The war around them was erupting to newer, more bitter levels; but there would be no more fighting within the walls of their home. The Monroes were united again. It was a pity it had taken a looming and indefinite separation to bring about the peace in their family.

"I'm going to miss you, Papa," she quavered against his shoulder. Her heart ached already.

"Not half as much as I will miss you," Jack Senior muttered into her hair. "Look after your brothers, my precious girl."

"I will, Papa."

"I'll come for the three of you the moment the war is over."

Her shoulders shook as her emotions overtook her. It was a promise they both knew he might not be able to keep. Nevertheless, she would be praying day and night that he would do exactly that.

THE NEXT MORNING, Papa and Jackson rode with Anna Kate, Will, and Grady to the train depot in their family's stately carriage. She tried not to chuckle as her younger brothers groaned and complained about the number of travel bags and trunks their housekeeper, Tanya, had helped her pack. She knew their biggest fear was that they might be stuck helping her lug them the rest of the way. *Mercy me!* Of all the people she was leaving behind, she would sorely miss the maternal, doting attentions of Tanya Cunningham. She was more than hired help. She was a widow who had more or less adopted their family as her own and treated them as such. Anna Kate had made the woman promise at least a dozen times to take care of Papa and Jackson in her absence.

"This is it." Mr. Monroe rapped smartly on the wall of the carriage to indicate where he wanted their driver, Felix, to halt.

Anna Kate had never been fond of goodbyes, but she was especially dreading this one. "Don't say it," she choked as Jackson enveloped her in a gigantic hug. They'd always been close, like two peas in a pod. This was going to be their longest separation to date. "Don't say one blessed thing that will make me cry again, else I'll never forgive you."

"I didn't intend to," he grumbled. "I was only going to urge you to keep your guard up against any and all unscrupulous rogues of the male species in my absence."

"I declare," she teased, her spirits rising several degrees at the underlying affection in his words. "I might actually find a beau if you're not around to threaten bodily harm to every gentleman who dares to look in my direction."

He flicked her nose affectionately. "Just fulfilling my brotherly responsibilities. You're as pretty as a peach, Anna Kate. Everyone east of the Mississippi knows it, and everybody west is about to find out." Though he kept his tone of voice light, he looked genuinely concerned.

She flushed in appreciation. "Says the charming bachelor with the mile-long line of wishful debutantes batting their lashes at you every day of the week."

"Pshaw!" He gave her a look of sheer disgust and rolled his eyes.

"I'm right," she jibed, "which you're making no effort to deny."

"Go, minx." He gave her a playful shove. "Go, before I change my mind and send Frederick with you."

"Heaven forbid!" She did not have to fake the shudder that worked its way through her.

Thanks to Jackson's teasing, Will and Grady's squabbling, and her father becoming distracted by a business associate who was passing by, Anna Kate was able to board the train with dry eyes. Her heart was full of a dozen unspoken fears and worries, though.

She drew a deep breath as she stepped inside the dining car where they would begin their journey. Momentarily closing her eyes to collect her emotions, she promptly bumped into something warm and solid. "Oomph!" Her hands flew out, and her eyelids snapped open. She found herself staring into the amused dark eyes of a handsome, broad-shouldered stranger. His tall frame was folded compactly into a black suit, a gold paisley waistcoat like the kind she'd been trying so hard to get Frederick to wear, and a snowy dress shirt with a bolo. The brim of his Stetson was pulled rakishly low.

Oh, my! Her heartbeat quickened at the realization she'd gone and run into her first honest-to-heavens cowboy before leaving Atlanta. It was both unexpected and a thousand shades of wonderful. Ignoring the vague twinge of concern about why a man his age wasn't wearing a military uniform, she treated him to one of her most ladylike smiles — one that was both gracious and apologetic. She did not wish to appear overeager or starved for company, though she certainly was.

"My apologies, sir." Her voice held a breathless quality that had nothing to do with the jolt of their impact and everything to do with his towering frame and nearness. Their proximity incidentally treated her to a delightful whiff of his aftershave, which further underscored his sheer maleness.

"Pardon me, ma'am." He tipped his hat at her and shot her a lopsided grin that sent a delicious shiver through her midsection. "Please assure me you're none the worse for our collision."

Mercy, but he was handsome in a tanned, outdoorsy way, though his baritone held a puzzling hint of the north. It wasn't the accent she would have expected of a man returning west. Unless he'd entered the dining car by mistake, however, that was exactly where he was heading.

"I am quite fine, Mr. Ah…" Perhaps it was forward of her, flirtatious even, but Anna Kate was dying to know the man's name and why she'd not previously met him. Her family was acquainted with just about every noteworthy person in Atlanta, so she was certain they'd never before been introduced. Was he merely passing through Atlanta on business? Would they be riding together on the train for long? She suddenly hoped so!

"Gregory Armstrong, ma'am." He held out a large hand.

"Pleased to meet you, Mr. Armstrong." What a gorgeous name! No, she couldn't think of any Armstrongs living in Atlanta. He must be passing through, then. She intended to simply touch her fingers to his, but he enveloped her slender hand with his much larger one and gave it a firm shake.

"I, ah…am Anna Kate Monroe." She deplored the hitch of hesitation in her voice, wondering where her lifetime of southern aplomb had flown to.

"The pleasure is all mine, Miss Monroe." He boldly lifted her fingers to brush his hard mouth lazily across her knuckles.

Good gracious! I beg to differ. She had to dig deep to summon enough poise to quell another shiver of delight. Her sadness at leaving home dimmed considerably beneath the prospect of traveling with such a mysterious and charming stranger, one with an utterly delicious sounding name.

Gregory Armstrong. She repeated his name in her head, hearing the hint of northern starch in it all over again.

Maybe Papa and Jackson were right. Maybe it was time to take a break from the war-riddled south. Though it was a thousand shades of frivolous and silly of her, she was already hoping that the fascinating cowboy who was oh-so-slowly lowering her hand would be around for a decent leg of the journey.

I hope you enjoyed this excerpt from
Lawfully Witnessed.
Available now in eBook, paperback and Kindle Unlimited at Amazon!

Much love,
Jovie

ALSO BY JOVIE

For the most up-to-date printable list of my sweet historical books:

Click here

or go to:

https://www.jografford.com/joviegracebooks

For the most up-to-date printable list of my sweet contemporary books:

Click here

or go to:

https://www.JoGrafford.com/books

ABOUT JOVIE

Jovie Grace is an Amazon bestselling author of sweet and inspirational historical romance books full of faith, family, and second chances. She also writes sweet contemporary romance as Jo Grafford.

Free Book!

Visit www.JoGrafford.com to sign up for my New Release Newsletter and receive a FREE copy of one of my sweet romance stories!

1.) Follow on Amazon!
amazon.com/author/jografford

2.) Join Cuppa Jo Readers!
https://www.facebook.com/groups/CuppaJoReaders

3.) Follow on Bookbub!
https://www.bookbub.com/authors/jo-grafford

4.) Follow on Instagram!

https://www.instagram.com/jografford/

- amazon.com/authors/jo-grafford
- bookbub.com/authors/jo-grafford
- facebook.com/JovieGraceBooks
- instagram.com/jografford
- pinterest.com/jografford

Made in United States
Orlando, FL
07 January 2024